Right, that's it, I thought. Ideal time to test my no-Kalmasol trick. I spoke to the others after lights out.

'Let's all do it! Let's be drug-free for the day – our real selves.'

'Good God, man, we're barmy enough *on* the damn stuff!'

'Ah, c'mon, Rav, do you really wanna spend the rest of your life controlled by drugs? Let's show the world we don't need tranquillizing to be tranquil! Let's prove to ourselves we don't need dope to cope!'

'Ah, turn it off!' said Archie. 'I've gotta take me meds, or I might just burn the place down!'

'Crying out loud, guys,' I said. 'Let's take control! Just for a couple of days, that's all I'm asking.'

D1144012

NOODLE HEAD

JONATHAN KEBBE

CORGI BOOKS

NOODLE HEAD
A CORGI BOOK 978 0 552 55204 2 (from January 2007)
0 552 55204 6

Published in Great Britain by Corgi Books,
an imprint of Random House Children's Books

This edition published 2005

3 5 7 9 10 8 6 4 2

Papers used by Random House Children's Books are natural,
recyclable products made from wood grown in sustainable
forests. The manufacturing processes conform to the
environmental regulations of the country of origin.

Typeset in Sabon by Palimpsest Book Production Ltd,
Polmont, Stirlingshire

Corgi Books are published by
Random House Children's Books,
61–63 Uxbridge Road, London W5 5SA,
a division of The Random House Group Ltd,
in Australia by Random House Australia (Pty) Ltd,
20 Alfred Street, Milsons Point, Sydney, NSW 2061, Australia,
in New Zealand by Random House New Zealand Ltd,
18 Poland Road, Glenfield, Auckland 10, New Zealand,
and in South Africa by Random House (Pty) Ltd,
Isle of Houghton, Corner of Boundary Road & Carse O'Gowrie,
Houghton 2198, South Africa

THE RANDOM HOUSE GROUP Limited Reg. No. 954009
www.kidsatrandomhouse.co.uk

A CIP catalogue record for this book is available
from the British Library.

Printed and bound in Great Britain by
Cox & Wyman Ltd, Reading, Berkshire

To my sister Nicki with love

Acknowledgements

Marcus King would like to give a big hug and thank you to Shanthi Jacobs, Sean Neary, John Wall, Rory O'Leary and Rehana Malik for their invaluable assistance researching my story – and another big hug and thank you to Sue Cook, Kelly Cauldwell and Sophie Nelson for helping me tell it.

Prologue

Running is all I know. It's a game of survival – my survival, which is kind of important to me. The game turned nightmare when they picked me up in France again. *Les flics* weren't in the mood – no coffee and croissants this time. Back to Dover in handcuffs.

I apologized to the cop they sent over to fetch me. 'No sweat, mate,' he said. 'I enjoyed the crossing.'

I apologized to my mum and dad and got my ears burned. They understood my feelings about school, but the law is the law.

I apologized to the magistrate for taking up so many people's time, but he wasn't too cool about it.

'Marcus King,' he said, 'stand up.'

I stood up.

'I'm sending you to Dovedale Hall!'

Didn't sound too bad, Dovedale, but my social worker went pale. She tried to fight my corner, but the magistrate was having none of it. 'This has been going on for too long, and you' – pointing his specs at me – 'are going down for a period of not less than twelve months.'

You could see his point. I was fifteen and I'd been running away from school since I was five. The sight of a school, any school, makes me queasy. The smell makes me want to vomit. It's not a game to me. From back in Infants I had to get out, get as far away as possible; stay free for as long as possible. I used to run home. Then it'd be the park, then the shopping centre. I graduated to more serious stunts, running off to Hastings, Folkestone, Brighton, kipping in a sleeping bag, one eye open for trouble, washing people's cars or mowing their lawns for a few quid, shoplifting when desperate. I love the seaside – breezy air and open space, no one to tell me what to do. Hours spent composing song lyrics, tossing pebbles into the waves. I had friends everywhere – everybody knew me, even over in Calais and Dieppe. People thought I was seventeen, eighteen, and they'd call out, '*Ho, Marcus! Comment ça va?*' You couldn't miss me – tall, cool, red dreadlocks. Yeah, red! They call me Noodle Head. My dad's Jamaican – plays a mean sax; my mum's from the East End and has glorious red hair.

Don't get me wrong, I don't hate teachers, they're victims of the system too. I always got on well with my teachers. Most understood that I had to have the door open, which was a bit of a problem sometimes in winter. I'm like that anywhere. I need to see an open door. On the ferry over to France, if there wasn't an open door I'd stay out on deck whatever the weather. Car journeys can be a problem too. Used to drive my parents mad, having to stop all of a sudden to let me out.

But school was the worst, because school combines two horrors – being cooped up for hours on end, and being forced to do things you have no say in. I believe in democracy, I want a say in my life. I can't stand sitting at a desk hour after hour learning what the government has ordered teachers to teach me. Learn this and this and this, and we'll test you on it tomorrow. Imagine if they made sex compulsory, and threatened to test you regularly. That'd be it, nobody would want to have sex. It'd be the beginning of the end of the world. You've got to want to work, of your own free will. But school is all about control, and being controlled was the one thing I couldn't bear.

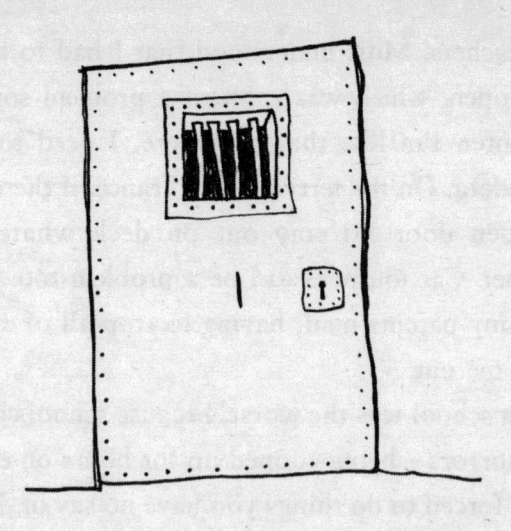

They say almost every boy cries his first night, and if he doesn't cry the first, he sure as hell cries the second. Doesn't matter how tough you think you are. Bury your face in your pillow, and nobody will hear . . .

Dovedale Hall – England's Alcatraz for teenage tearaways. You've probably heard of it – after what happened to me.

All the way up in the train I was shaking so hard, I made my minder shake, my leg against his, feet tapping with nerves. He kept throwing me looks – like, *Can't you keep still?* – but what was I supposed to do? Pretend we were off to the Seychelles? Then came the long car hike through wild winter scenery, my nerves shredding as ever smaller towns slipped by, until there was nothing left but isolated farms and houses. The road began to climb; snow began to fall.

'Tell us about this place,' I said.

'Well, it's not a holiday camp, mate.'

The car was sliding on the snowy road. The driver cursed and pulled over.

'May as well stretch our legs,' said my minder, as if we shared the one pair, and we got out and watched the driver wrestle a pair of snow chains onto the back wheels.

On we drove, the road climbing through silent woodland, wipers beating away fat flakes of snow. I insisted on having my window open, and nearly froze everybody to death.

I remember my first sight of the place as if it was yesterday. Our headlights picked out the sign – DOVEDALE HALL. The car slowed, found the turning. The road climbed an avenue of snow-coated trees, passed a cottage and turned into a wide forecourt. Dovedale Hall stood out against the night sky, huge with lighted windows. My home for the next twelve months. The car scrunched over gravel and shuddered to a stop. My minder got out, dragging me with him. It's a weird feeling being handcuffed to a stranger.

The front door opened; a tall man in a dark suit and white roll-neck stepped onto a stone porch, came down the steps and exchanged a few words with my minder, who unlocked the cuffs and handed me over with my suitcase and some paperwork. My hands were free, the two men were talking – I felt like bolting into the woods and running all night, but I was tired and disorientated, my mind tearing off at angles. I looked up at the house, massive against the sky. If they think they can keep me here, they're making a big mistake.

The tall man dropped a hand like a claw on my shoulder and said, 'Come inside.' He said it softly and kind of sad, like he'd seen my fate and it wasn't pretty. Still gripping my shoulder, he steered me up the steps into a high-ceilinged entrance hall tiled like a giant chessboard. It felt like stepping into one of those old films they show in the afternoon. From somewhere above came sounds of feet on wooden floors, furniture legs scraping.

He led me to a medical room, a mini ER with hospital beds, machines and monitors, where he let me go and faced me. He had hard eyes and a hatchet nose. Hair receding like a black tide. Reminded me of a bird of prey hovering in the blue – a lone predator.

'You've made me late,' he said.

I meant to say, *Sorry, I'd have told the driver to get a move on!* but I was too numb. And this man was dangerous – you could feel the vibes coming off him.

'I'm Mr Strang – we'll be seeing a good deal of each other, and it'll be in your interest to stay on my good side. As for that *hair*' – eyeing my dreadlocks – 'we'll see about that in the morning. Doctor?' he called out.

'Coming,' came a cheery voice from the next room.

'Empty your pockets, boy,' said the Predator.

I froze. My left-hand trouser pocket held my good-luck charms.

'I already emptied them for my minder.'

'Empty them again.'

Fumbling with one pocket at a time, I tried stalling – 'Amazing place you got here . . . I've hardly ever seen snow.'

'Your hand, boy, your left hand,' said Mr Strang, and I had no choice but to slowly open it, and there in the palm lay three small stones, polished velvety-smooth by millions of rolling waves, each stone a different shape and shade of white and gold, with dimples and grooves for restless fingers to caress. 'They're nothing, sir, just some old pebbles from Brighton beach. I like feeling them – they help me concentrate on my work.'

'Bin.'

'Sorry?'

'B–I–N, *bin*,' he repeated, pointing.

Desperate, I kind of idled towards the bin. At that moment, the doctor breezed in from the next room in a white coat. While the Predator had a quiet word with him, I dropped the three pebbles loudly in the bin – and scooped them up again.

'Right, Mr King, this is Dr Cavendish. You'll do precisely what he says. Any trouble and you'll answer to me.'

'I don't give trouble, sir.'

'Glad to hear it.'

'Sir . . . ?'

'Goodnight, Mr King.'

'About the dreadlocks – they're totally harmless and if you don't mind . . .'

He was gone. I turned to meet the doctor. Short and stout with silvery hair and big owl specs, he was flicking through my file.

'How are you feeling?'

'Pretty good, thanks, Doc,' I said, scared out of my wits.

'A persistent truant, I understand.'

'Conscientious objector, Doc.'

'A record-breaking runaway.'

'More of an explorer.'

'Any childhood illnesses?'

'Obstinacy?'

'Or allergies?'

'School.'

'Sit down and roll up your sleeve.'

'Any particular reason?'

'I'm going to take your pulse and blood pressure.'

He was pointing at a stool. The worn and cracked plastic cover really worried me. Couldn't help thinking of all the guys who must have sat on it before me, wondering what lay ahead. He pumped up my arm, humming cheerfully. Handed me a paper cup, in it a little blue pill marked KM, and I said, 'What's this?' and he said, 'Something to calm you down,' and I said, 'Do I look like somebody who needs calming down?'

He handed me a second cup, containing water. 'It's low dose and perfectly safe – nothing to worry about.'

'Listen, Doc, if that's Kalmasol, they've stuck me on it before and I really don't get on with it.'

'Relax, my friend. It's specially formulated to reduce stress and hyperactivity.'

'Actually, it's not, Doc. It was concocted years ago for something totally different. I know, because I checked it out on the web. I'm sorry, but that stuff gives me the shakes.'

'Take it for now, dear boy, and we'll discuss it in the morning.'

I was too whacked and strung out to resist. I juggled the pill in my hand and sipped it down.

'Excellent chap! Mr Litner?' the doctor called out.

In the doorway stood a bloke a year or two older than me, lean, pale and wearing a black dressing gown and slippers.

'Vinny Litner will show you to your dormitory. Don't forget your suitcase, Malcolm. Goodnight.'

'Goodnight, Doc, and it's Marcus,' I said, but he was gone.

The bloke in the black robe was looking at me like I just crawled out of a drain. His face was all bone, mouth thin as a blade. A jerk of the head told me to follow him.

'Yo! Nice to meet you.' I threw out a hand as I tried to keep up along a gloomy corridor. 'I'm Marcus King. You're Vinny Litner, right?'

He looked straight ahead – not a word.

'What do you do here anyway? What's with the black gear?'

Nothing. I was dirt on his shoes.

'Listen, it's OK, if you're in one of those silent religious orders, that's cool, just nod or—'

Shake your head, I was going to say, when he shoved me in the shoulder and pointed a finger in my face. '*Toff* – that's all you need to know, boy.'

'Toff?'

'Short for Trusted Offender – with special responsibilities.'

'Oh cool, like a sheriff!'

'There are four of us toffs and you never, ever speak to us 'less we speak to you first – got it?'

He was from my part of the world, same South London accent, filed to a sharper edge.

'That's your last warning,' he said.

'Don't I get a *first* warning?'

He raised his fist.

'All right, I got it!' I flinched. 'Those were the last words I'll speak unless spoken to first . . . honest . . . except of course for the ones I'm speaking now, promising that these are the last words I'll speak unless—'

A fist caught me between the eyes and I went down, covering my head as the kicking started.

'Yo! Vinny,' I croaked, 'what's a nice guy like you doing in a—?'

'What the devil's going on?' A deep voice from the landing above.

'Teaching the new slog manners, Mr Trust,' replied Vinny.

'Clean him up.'

Vinny tossed me half a toilet roll. 'Well good for you I've only these on,' he said, meaning his ridiculous carpet slippers.

'Lucky me!' I agreed, marvelling at the blood coming from my nose.

'Get upstairs.'

I went ahead, suitcase in one hand, bog roll pressed to my face in the other.

'Oi, Vinny' – over my shoulder – 'ever considered one of those anger-management gigs?'

'Lucky it's your first day, boy,' he hissed back, and shoved me through an open door. 'This is your poxy coop and these are your poxy coopmates. Get washed and bedded down. And hurry up, the rest of you,' he ordered.

'Thanks, Vinny, you're a gentleman!' I called after him, and turned to find three youths staring at me. One was tall, pale and handsome; one a huge smirking Indian; the third a shifty-looking skinhead.

I put the suitcase down, mopped blood from my nose.

'Nice place you got here! Cool colour scheme, kind of phlegm and cyanide-blue – I like it.'

They gazed at me.

'You dudes look a million laughs,' I said, stepping into the centre of the room. 'Can't wait to get to know you better – though I can see it won't be easy getting a word in.'

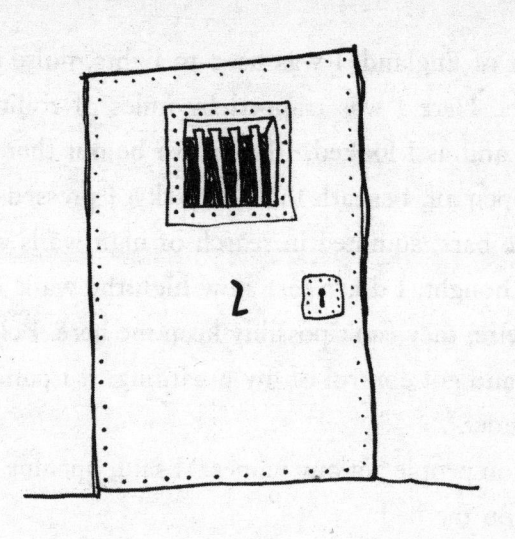

They stared at me like I was a disease. I was shaking – I wasn't used to violence. I never had enemies at school. Sure there's always the odd racial dig, kids jockeying for position and all that crap. Someone threatens me, I generally jump back, throw up my hands – *Whoa, bro, take it slow! What we fighting for?* Nobody ever laid that kind of hate on me, not like Vinny Litner, and I couldn't stop trembling.

The dormitory – or *coop* – had four beds, each with its own chest of drawers and chair. The only vacant bed was under the high, barred window with the wind whistling through. Bars on the window! The sight of them tore the breath from my throat. I went over and grasped them in my two fists and looked out at frozen trees, hills and sky – and beyond that more frozen trees, hills, sky. It was mid-January somewhere in the far north of England. I was used to lights, noise and city streets. Here I was trapped by miles of rolling darkness, and as I looked, I longed to be out there; out in the open air, beneath the starry sky. I pressed my face to the bars, squinted in search of high walls and wire and thought, I don't care how high the walls or sharp the wire, they can't possibly keep me here. I closed my eyes and got control of my breathing. If I panicked I'd go under.

'You people got any names?' I said, opening my suitcase on the bed.

'I wouldn't . . .'

I looked up. It was the skinhead.

'You wouldn't what?'

'Pick that bed.'

'Do I get a choice?'

'Last lodger topped himself,' he said in a raw, high-pitched voice like a saw snagged in wood.

A shiver went through me – his hollow gaze.

'That's nice to know,' I said. 'Gimme a dead boy's bed every time.'

They were all looking at me, wary of their new coopmate. I tried to focus on my unpacking, but the skinhead had peeled my nerves and I said, casual-like, 'I suppose they lock the door at night?'

Suddenly the room was spinning and I felt violently ill. I weaved towards the corridor, saw bright light and gravitated towards it, stumbled down some steps into a blinding bathroom, around the wash basins to the nearest toilet cubicle, fell on my knees and vomited the universe. Collapsed on the tiles and lay there.

Footsteps and jangling keys.

'*Holy Moses*, what the devil . . . ?'

The voice of God was looking down at me. He was broad, black and muscled, with a shaved cannonball head. A big bunch of keys swung from his belt. He wore a shiny black jumpsuit, gold earring and a look of extreme doubt, like he'd come across his share of hopeless cases, but I took the trophy.

'What's the matter, boy – are you ill?'

'It's the drugs,' I said. 'I told him this'd happen.'

'You smell evil, boy,' growled Moses.

'Not me,' I said, getting up off the floor.

'We're all born with sin and you look brimful to me.'

I looked him in the eye. 'You can keep your sin – I don't buy it.'

'Who do you think you are, boy?' he said, bearing down on me, eyes blazing.

'Marcus King. And you?'

'Clarence Trust. Get naked,' he said, and chucked a washbag at me. My washbag!

'Pardon?'

Pointing at the showers – 'Use every drop of shampoo. I'll be back in five.'

He hung a towel on a hook and left. I stripped and picked one of four showers. Shampoo smelling like toilet cleaner squirted out of an unmarked bottle. I tried all four showers, but the water had two temperatures: cold and ice-cold. My flesh howled – my dreadlocks recoiled like snakes from fire. I heard Moses returning and turned my back; I shampooed my head, torso and privates, all the time keeping a fixed smile, like – *This is cool, I could get into this.*

'That'll do.'

I stepped away and he handed me the towel. Rolled his sleeve and switched off the water. Pointed at a pair of regulation pyjamas – bright orange – and a tatty pair of grandad slippers, same as Vinny Litner wore.

'Three minutes to get your backside into bed. Reading time and then lights out. You'll find a best-seller in your top drawer. Read it, boy. Your salvation lies within.'

I put on the pyjamas and slippers, brushed my teeth and returned to the coop, where everyone was getting ready for bed. Still shivering, I tested a thick pipe running along the foot of a wall. It was warm and I sat on it. Then I checked out my chest of drawers. Two top drawers – one with a Bible in it – and two bigger drawers lined with old newspaper.

'Shelly,' somebody said.

It was the handsome dude, getting into the bed opposite.

'Shelly,' he repeated, his accent Welsh, his tone gloomy, 'is my *name*.'

'Nice to meet you, Shelly,' I said, going over to shake his hand.

'Nobody in here topped himself,' he answered, nodding at my bed. 'He tried, that's all.'

I glanced across the aisle at Skinhead, who was scratching an armpit and grinning at me.

'Name's Marcus,' I said. 'Friends call me Noodle Head.'

They looked at me like I was nuts.

'Right . . .' smiled the Welsh hunk.

'Yes, very good!' said the Indian sumo wrestler. 'Very tasty too!'

The skinhead kind of frowned – he didn't get it.

'His *hair*, Ratso,' said Shelly, rolling his eyes.

Ratso gave Shelly the finger and grinned crazily. 'We're all noodle heads in here, case you forgot.'

I was wondering what exactly Ratso meant when my Indian neighbour introduced himself with a theatrical flourish: 'Ravi the First of Rajisthan!'

'Pleased to meet you, Ravi,' I said, and shook the hand of the youth who was so wondrously massive his bed sagged.

'You may address me as *Your Majesty*.'

'Flasher's his name,' said Skinhead.

Skinhead – or Ratso – was standing bare-chested, staring at me. He hadn't had taken his eyes off me since the minute I walked in. He appeared to have scorched his eyebrows off, and had a menacing wasp tattooed on each shoulder, swarms of locusts on his arms.

'And you are . . . ?' I said.

'Sod off.'

'Unusual name.'

'*Sod . . . off*,' he repeated, nice and clear, pulling his covers over his head.

'Don't mind him, he's bonkers!' said Ravi.

I laughed and got into bed. Crisp sheets and grey blankets, no comfy duvets here.

'Ratso is the illustrious gentleman's name!' said Flasher, his accent Indian and superbly posh. 'And never was a title more aptly applied.'

'One of these dark nights, Flasher,' said Ratso, running a finger across his throat, 'I'm gonna slit your gizzard.'

Ravi smiled, hand on heart. 'Such charming sentiments . . . such immaculate manners.'

'Chop you up and flog you for dog food.'

'Dear God – isn't it bad enough sharing living quarters with malodorous commoners, without being cooped up with a psychopathic nincompoop?'

'Even when we get out of here, Flasher, you'll have no place to hide.'

I shivered, wrapped my dreadlocks in my towel and lay back, praying someone would hurry up and kill the light so I could try and sleep. My face and head throbbed from Vinny's fist and feet – what a treat to think I'd be seeing so much more of him from now on. I noticed the lad who called himself Shelly observing me from behind a book. He alone seemed detached, composed.

I said again, 'So, do they lock this door at night?'

'Don't be stupid – 'course they do,' said Ratso.

I turned over and closed my eyes, bracing myself for a night of hell.

'He's winding you up. Coops are never locked,' said Shelly. 'Fire regulations.'

I sighed secretly with relief.

Moses was back. 'Settle down, not a whisper,' he rumbled, flicking a switch and plunging the coop into darkness. 'God is nigh. Prepare yourselves.'

His steps faded up some stairs. Night one had begun and I lay stiff with fear. I was used to the pulse of the city, getting together with friends to make music. I was used to raiding the fridge day or night, chatting to my mum, hanging out with my dad. Do these people who lock you up ever stop to think what it might feel like – torn from family, friends, your usual beat? Shipped north to the farthest corner of England, banged up in the middle of nowhere.

What am I doing here? Why can't they leave me alone? What difference does it make if a handful of free-thinkers excuse themselves from school and make their own way in the world? Is England going to disappear beneath the waves because Marcus King can't stand a stuffy classroom and would rather chill out on the beach?

You can't keep me here. This is a free country and I'm a free man.

Just then, as I lay rolling with my thoughts, shadows entered the coop and fell across my bed. I recognized Vinny Litner at once. He had someone with him, a hefty geezer with pockmarked face and piggy eyes. Both carried big, spiky hairbrushes, a popular choice of weapon in Dovedale, as I found out later, known as *hedgehogs*.

'Vinny, what's the—?'

Story, I was going to say, when a flurry of fists to the head stunned me, and when I came to, they had turned me over on my front with my pyjama bottoms pulled down. While his sidekick held me down, Vinny hog-whipped me. I tried to struggle free, but these thugs were eighteen-year-olds and strong. I tried not to cry out, but by the time they swapped round and the big yob took his turn, my bum was on fire and they had to stuff a pillow in my mouth to shut me up. All the time it was happening, my coopmates listened in silence.

After the raiders had gone, I got up and stood there, trembling in the dark. 'I can't thank you enough . . . the way you all jumped to my aid. What a stroke of luck to be cooped up with such friggin' heroes.'

I stood looking out at the winter sky, fighting back the tears and vowing to get even. To get even and to *get out*. So began my first night in Dovedale Finishing School for Exceptionally Gifted Boys.

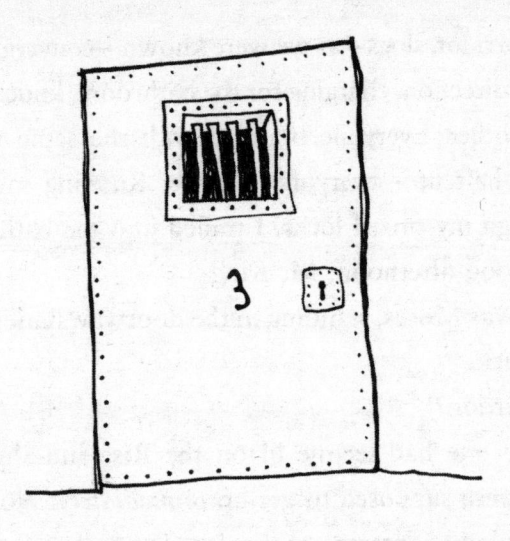

After the hog-whipping episode, I slept feverishly, clutching my three Brighton pebbles. Woke suddenly before dawn. A clock above the door, lit by a dim nightlight, said 6.25 a.m. Man, was it cold, the air outside the covers arctic! I turned over and went back to sleep for a few seconds.

Next thing I knew the mother and father of alarms was blasting me awake. It was 6.30 a.m. – lights blazing, groans and curses ringing out as figures rose from their beds like ghosts from graves. The alarm went on and on, and was so loud and piercing that for days after I woke early to be ready for it.

I didn't know what was going on. My coopmates were in motion, falling out of bed into waiting slippers, Shelly first through the door, Ravi and Ratso staggering after him. Moving as in a dream, I joined the stampede along the corridor, slogs – as we were known – converging from every direction, charging for the bathroom, knocking into each other. Everyone branded with the same viciously short haircut – everyone but me. Running my fingers through my prized locks, I trailed into the bathroom.

'Good afternoon, Mr King.'

It was Moses, standing in the doorway, hands behind his back.

'Pardon?'

No one had let me in on the Rise-and-Shine rule. You were supposed to get up *immediately*. No time to stretch and contemplate the day. The bell rang for sixty seconds, and if you weren't inside the bathroom when it stopped, Moses nabbed you.

'Back to base, Mr King,' he said, and ushered me back to the coop. 'One hundred and fifty press-ups!'

I swore under my breath.

'There *is* devil in you, boy,' he said.

'No, boss,' I smiled, getting down to start my press-ups, 'there's no devil in me.'

Each time I flagged, he told me to breathe deep and keep going. When I was finally done, he told me to get up and handed me a cup of water and my regulation tracksuit – orange again, with a black stripe down the crease of the arms and legs. Then he escorted me down to the dining hall, where it was 7.05 and I'd missed breakfast.

'Reject the darkness in your soul, son,' Moses rumbled

in my ear as he handed me over to the waiting doctor. 'Leave your door open for the Lord.'

'I'll do my best,' I said, and faced the smiling doctor.

Dr Cavendish – or Dr Doughnut, as he was known – was waiting for me by his trolley. Turned out he was an experienced Child and Adolescent Consultant Psychiatrist. Normally you never see these guys, they keep their distance, but Dovedale's drug regime was considered too important to be left in the hands of mere mortals, so old Doughnut's mug and medical bag were ever present.

He was holding out a little paper cup containing a little blue pill.

'Don't tell me—'

'It's for your own good, Malcolm.'

'It's Marcus, and I told you, Doc, Kalmasol does my head in.'

'You may notice mild side-effects, but they won't last.'

'It makes me feel real weird, and in any case I like to be in control – know what I mean?'

'Open up now, there's a good lad.'

'What's going on?' A voice at my back.

It was him – dark suit, white roll-neck – the Predator.

'I hope you're not giving the doctor any trouble, Mr King.'

'Just wondering if we could discuss this, Mr Strang.'

'There's nothing to discuss. Every slog takes his daily medicine. Misbehave and the dosage rises.'

'So I don't get a choice?'

'Yes, you do. You can take it voluntarily, or we can call security and administer it by force.'

I returned the Predator's merciless gaze. Held out my hand. Dr Doughnut handed me the pill and water. I put the pill in my mouth and washed it down.

'Show, dear boy!' said the doctor.

'Sorry?'

'Open your mouth, there's a good chap,' he said, lifted my chin and peered in.

'Follow me,' said Mr Strang, and led me from the room. 'Be grateful for the medication. Your stay here will be a lot calmer, your chances of getting into trouble significantly reduced.'

'I don't like being out of control,' I replied.

'You're out of control already, Mr King – that's why you're here.'

He took me to a gym, where a visiting barber waited, wearing a shiny barber's jacket the colour of dried blood. Pointed me onto a tall stool.

'The usual, Mr Strang?' enquired the barber.

The Predator nodded.

'Excuse me, sir, could we talk about this?'

'There's nothing to talk about, Mr King.'

'With respect, sir, I'm being relieved of twelve months of my life and I'm not arguing with that. But the magistrate said nothing about relieving me of my hair.'

'As long as you're in Dovedale, Mr King, you'll submit

to Dovedale's rules and regulations. Failure to be seated by the time I count to three, and your twelve-month sentence will spontaneously grow a supplementary limb.'

I looked into his cold blue eyes. He started to count. 'One . . . two . . .'

I climbed onto the stool, back straight, eyes level. I could feel the Kalmasol entering my blood. The barber selected his biggest scissors – gave them a smart shine. I closed my eyes.

Snip-snip-snip – this bloke couldn't please his gaffer fast enough.

'Ah, c'mon, leave me a roof over my head!' I said. 'My hair's my *signature*! My *credentials*! I don't believe this . . .'

I can't explain why it felt like torture. It didn't hurt, but it cut deep.

The scissors paused, the Predator nodded. My hair lay around my feet like a blood-stained carpet. The barber shoved a mirror in my face. The dude in the mirror was no dude, but a fool with a big head and ears and a red skullcap and I thought, Don't I know you from somewhere?

The barber was delighted with himself. 'That's more like it, don't you agree?'

'Amazing,' I said. 'You're an artist.' I touched my head – it felt like a doormat, and I thought, That's what they want, a doormat.

'Over here,' the Predator ordered, and made me stand

against a bare wall while he aimed a camera at me and took a set of official photos. I looked straight into the camera's eyes.

I'm not a criminal – *I am not a criminal* . . .

On the outside I stayed cool; inside I was torched, and for days after I felt terrible, like in those dreams where everyone's looking at you because you're stark naked. Meanwhile, after the dreadlock massacre, Mr Strang marched me out the back door of the gym into the cold. My tracksuit was thick, but not that thick. An icy wind carrying pins of sleet whipped across a rugby field. Around the field trudged scores of slogs puffing white breath, hounded by a member of staff – known as a whip – and all wearing the same orange gear with black stripes, like a plague of wasps. Every slog wore his tracksuit hood over his close-cropped head, like the opening scene of a boot-camp movie.

The whip yelling at them and leaning on a cane was short and stocky with cropped, spiky hair and a weathered face – my first sight of Mr Ledpace, or Harry Headcase, former sergeant-major in some crack regiment, invalided out of the army after some accident and bitter as the wind.

'Every boy does twenty laps of the pitch after breakfast,' Mr Strang informed me. 'To apologize for your insolence, you'll oblige me with forty.'

'Sir, I didn't get any breakfast.'

'You obviously weren't up in time.'

'I wasn't familiar with the sixty-second rule.'

'Ignorance may be bliss out there,' he said, nodding somewhere beyond the tree line, 'but in here it's an offence.'

I pulled on my hood and joined the fun, rubbing a Brighton pebble in the palm of my hand. The Kalmasol was kicking in, making me nauseous and sluggish. Originally hatched to control epileptic fits, it turned out better at suppressing anxiety and aggression. Scientists and doctors didn't know how it worked, and still don't. All they know is that it tinkers with the brain and generally has the desired effect.

I ran, head down, into the wind. The ground was white and hard, splattered here and there with breakfasts freshly vomited. Slogs were spread all round the pitch, some sleek and quick, others struggling. Among the slickers was Vinny Litner, cruising along with the pig-eyed thug who attacked me last night. Squinting into the wind, I spotted my coopmate Ravi bumbling along and caught him up.

'Who's the goon running with Skinny Hitler?'

'With *who*?' gasped Ravi, clutching an inhaler.

'Vinny Litner.'

'Ah! Liam *Strangeboy* Bland . . . another toff . . . Take my advice . . .'

I jogged beside him, awaiting his wisdom. He shook his head, too breathless to deliver. 'Keep . . . out . . . their way.'

By the third lap I was feeling dizzy. The Kalmasol was kicking in hard. My head felt like a hollowed-out coconut. I wanted to lift it off my neck and look inside. My whole body was feeling the effects, my limbs lazy and detachable. Just thirty-seven laps to go. Hang loose, string it out, I was thinking, when someone's foot caught me from behind and I crashed to the ground. I looked up to see Skinny Hitler and Strangeboy Bland overtaking me, running backwards and grinning.

'Who's got a new hair-do?'

'Oh, you noticed?' I smiled.

As I picked myself up and ran on, I thought, Laugh all you like, but I'm getting out of here . . . *I'm getting out.*

Harry Headcase sat on a box marked FIRST AID, ticking off each slog's lap count on a clipboard. Slogs finished and dragged themselves indoors, and soon there were only two of us left – Ravi sucking his inhaler and me. My face stung with cold, my hands and ears were frozen, my legs driftwood. Ravi, whom I'd overtaken several hundred times, sank to his knees. I saw from a distance that he was crying and went to his aid.

'Up you get, Your Majesty.'

'I can't . . .' he wheezed, latching onto me.

'Leave him alone!' yelled Sir.

'He's not well,' I yelled back, half dead myself.

Harry Headcase jumped up and ran at me, limping

on his stick. 'Are you deaf? Only here five minutes and stirring it already!'

'Yo! Sir, slow down – you're all strung out—'

'*Strung out?* Do you think I enjoy freezing my onions while you brats trot round like a bunch of fairies!'

'My sympathies, sir, but this bloke's in no fit state to do twenty laps.'

'*Twenty?* Who said anything about *twenty*?' he bawled. 'Flasher's not doing twenty because, soft-hearted sucker that I am, I permit him every morning to do – wait for it! – *ten*! He's done nine, so by my arithmetic, he's got about fifty metres to go . . . if that's all right with you?'

Hauling himself drunkenly to his feet, Ravi flung away an empty inhaler and limped into the mist. Sir checked his clipboard.

'Three laps left,' he informed me. 'You've got precisely nine minutes, or you'll start another ten.'

No time to argue – I stumbled on, running on virtual legs, rapping aloud to keep my mind distracted. '*Hey! Mr Predator, for pity's sake, Shaving my head was a big mistake . . .*'

Two laps to go – you can do it.

'*My locks were my ID, my individuALITY! You gone and done a crime against humANITY!*'

The thirty-ninth lap was the worst – the dope, the cold, the exhaustion.

'You're leaving it tight, boy – two minutes forty-nine for your last lap!'

Don't sound so happy! I wanted to say, but staggered on.

Sir was on his feet as I turned the last corner.

'Ten seconds . . . nine . . . eight . . . seven . . .'

Harry and his walking stick swam before my eyes. I was sure I'd done it – give or take a second or two – but as I reached him, clutching myself like a man with a bullet in his back, he was shaking his head.

'Failed!'

'What?'

'Ten more laps. I warned you, didn't I?' He chuckled reasonably. '*Move!*'

I stood bent double, looking at him. I'm not in the least violent, but not even the Kalmasol could stop me wanting to brain him with his own cane. I straightened up, fighting for air. If the plan was to break me, it was working. I shuffled on, determined to keep going. Better to die in the snow than be beaten by this ranting psycho. If I had to, I'd run for ever. What was to stop me anyway? There was no fence or wall that I could see, only miles and miles of trees, rock and hills. I soon discovered *that* was the problem – forty or fifty miles of it.

Dimly, as I limped along the try line, I became aware of thundering feet and glanced round to catch sight of a dozen senior slogs in rugby kit, led by Skinny Hitler and Strangeboy Bland, exchanging passes, swanking it up.

'State of him!' they jeered at me.

I hobbled on – a rugby ball struck me in the back of the head. No big deal – except in my condition it felt like being singled out by a ground-to-air missile and I hit the deck and lay there, until Harry Headcase lifted me up and shook me, his grinning followers looking on.

'Drink!' he ordered, shoving a bottle of water at me. I took a swig and choked.

'Let me introduce myself, sonny,' he said. 'My name is Mr Ledpace, Dovedale Hall's Health and Fitness Co-ordinator. When you're in my charge, you do as I say, and jump to it when I say it. If you can manage to remember that, you and I need never cross swords again – you follow? Good. Now, as a token of goodwill – to welcome you, as it were – I'm going to save you further pain. Go tidy your personal bed space in readiness for inspection.'

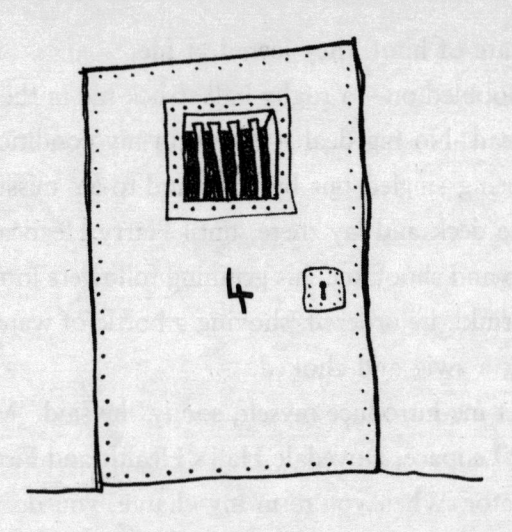

I returned, shivering, to the coop, where someone was waiting at the window, hands behind his back – Mr Strang.

'Not an auspicious start, Mr King.'

I wasn't sure what auspicious meant, but took his word for it. I was done in, feet blistered, legs mangled, head weirdly Kalmasoled, but I stood straight and looked him in the eye. He pointed at my chest of drawers.

'Everything onto the bed.'

I emptied my drawers. The Predator worked fast, making two piles. He declared the left-hand pile *prohibited* – rap magazine, radio, fountain pen, magnetic chess set, chewing gum and even Email, my ridiculous thumb-sized fighter-pilot mouse – complete with goggles, leather jacket and fur collar which my kid sister Clem gave me for my tenth birthday and my mum must have slipped into my suitcase.

'No frills here, boy,' he said, stuffing the forbidden items into a plastic bag marked M. KING – 307. 'They'll be returned when you leave.'

'Fountain pen?' I queried.

'A potential weapon.'

'Fair enough, sir, but my mouse wouldn't hurt a fly.'

'Don't be silly – how old are you?'

My sister gave it me, I wanted to say, but let it drop.

'And that bracelet comes off.'

I hesitated. My dad had given it me. 'It's special to me . . . if you don't mind.'

'No adornments.'

I removed it and handed it over. My head felt bare without my locks – my wrist bare without the bracelet. This can't go on, I thought – this cannot go on.

'Get dressed,' he said, pointing to my Dovedale uniform hanging by my bed. He stood waiting with my bag of confiscated possessions. I dressed quickly – black trousers and blazer, orange turtleneck sweater – no escaping orange – black socks and black slip-on shoes. The crest on the top pocket of the blazer featured a white dove in flight above a menacing red snake, and the words CARPE OCCASIONEM.

'Time to meet the Director, Mr King.'

'I took you, sir, for the Director,' I said, following him out.

Down the stairs and across the chessboard entrance hall we went, down a main corridor and past a door marked M. STRANG – DEPUTY DIRECTOR, stopping finally at an open door marked L. RICE-BIRD – DIRECTOR. Mr Strang knocked rapidly and stepped away.

'Come in,' said a voice – reassuring and female.

I went in. A woman sat behind a desk.

'Laura Rice-Bird,' the boss introduced herself, reaching out a hand without standing.

I leaned across and shook it.

'Welcome to Dovedale Hall, Marcus.'

I stood, hands behind my back, grateful the door was open. Laura Rice-Bird smiled at me. She was beautiful in an overcooked kind of way. I wondered what she'd look like without the fake tan and make-up. She wore heels and a black trouser suit – blonde hair scraped back. She was known, it turned out, as the Iceberg.

'How was your journey, Marcus?'

'Very pleasant, thank you, Ms Rice-Bird.'

'You slept well?'

'Like a log.'

She spoke posh, with a sprinkling of *Coronation Street*.

'Do you find your accommodation satisfactory?'

'The views from the window are amazing.'

'You're being well looked after?'

'Everybody's been – what can I say? The only problem . . .'

She nailed me with her gaze. I hesitated.

'. . . is the medication.'

'I beg your pardon?'

'The drugs. They don't agree with me. And in any case, I prefer to be in control . . . you know, of my own behaviour.'

Putting on a pair of gold-rimmed reading glasses, she consulted a slim file and read out: '*Habitual truant . . . pathologically inclined to run away . . .*'

'That's just my point, miss. I run away sometimes—'

'*Sometimes?*'

'Well, quite a lot' – I sort of laughed – 'because I like to be in control . . . you know, of my destiny.'

'Your destiny?' she repeated.

My humour suddenly deserted me. 'Look, it's not that I don't want to learn – I love learning: science, biology, ecology . . . It's that *I* want do the learning – know what I'm saying? Not have someone out front doing it for me.'

'*Alarmingly hyperactive,*' she read.

'Me? No, I just have quite a bit of natural energy.'

'*Severe case of ADHD – Attention Deficit Hyperactivity Disorder.*'

'No, no! Forgive me, but that's such a lazy diagnosis. I just get upset sometimes when doors are closed – you know, when I don't get a say in my own life.'

She had her glasses off and was smiling. Something told me I'd blown it.

'*Persistent shoplifter*, Marcus. What have you to say about that?'

'Occasional, not persistent, and only in a tight spot.'

'The main thing is you're here now,' she said, sitting back. 'Dovedale enjoys an exceptional reputation. Over the last few years, we have set out to show that a carefully monitored programme of Discipline, Drugs and Direction – *the three Ds* – is the best way to reform and rehabilitate young offenders. We have every facility here to turn young lives around – sporting, educational and medical. It costs taxpayers a great deal and there are those who'd like to shut us down to save money. Happily there are many more – here and abroad – who are watching this ground-breaking experiment with great interest, and I'm proud to report that I'm regularly asked to lecture on the success of Dovedale and its Three Ds regime. So, young man, *welcome* the discipline and direction! *Embrace* the medication! It should keep your hyperactivity and irrational phobias in check. Any questions?'

'If I behave and work hard, can I come off the Kalmasol altogether?'

'You wouldn't be here, young man, if you didn't have serious problems that require sensible measures.'

'You mean there's no—?'

'You're very fortunate to have been selected for Dovedale,' she said, drawing my attention to a framed inscription on the wall. 'Read aloud, please.'

'*Dovedale Hall is dedicated to the reform and*

rehabilitation of troubled boys,' I read in my clearest voice, '*bringing order and discipline to their lives, helping them respect themselves and others, in order to return them to the community as useful citizens.*'

Well? her eyes demanded.

'It sounds . . . amazing.'

'Unfortunately we don't always succeed. All too many boys leave here to pursue a mindless life of drugs and crime. Will you be joining them?'

'Absolutely not.'

'You've been sent to us for a provisional period of twelve months,' she said, addressing the luckiest lad in the world. 'However, boys who make good progress are sometimes released after six. Follow the Dovedale motto,' she said, indicating the Latin inscription on my blazer pocket, 'and I've every confidence you may be one of them.'

'What's it mean, miss?'

'*Carpe occasionem* – grab this unique opportunity.'

Stepping smartly round the desk, she put out her hand and looked me in the eye.

'Don't let me down, Marcus.'

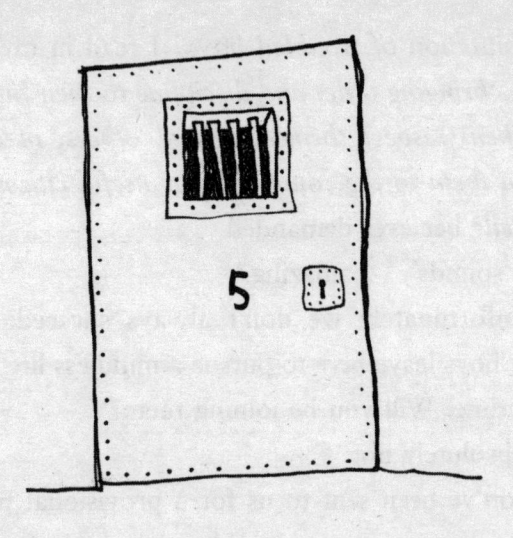

It could have been worse. Coops were never locked or closed, and classroom doors were often left open by teaching staff concerned for their own safety. Fire-escape doors were never locked for obvious reasons, and even the main front door had a huge key conveniently boxed beside it, in case of fire. Outside, there were no high walls laced with razor wire, no electric fences. Dovedale's grounds spread freely all around, tempting me to pretend I was on an outward-bound holiday.

Time and again, that first week, I collared different slogs with the same question – what's to stop us doing a runner? Answer: forty or fifty miles of rock, woods and wilderness to the nearest main road or railway. Not to mention a six-month extension to your sentence. Only one nutter had ever tried it, the legendary Tony

Trevino, who lasted twenty-four hours and was found nearly frozen less than a mile away. Probably thought he was halfway to London, but must have gone round in circles all night before a couple of tracker dogs found him. As well as stretching his sentence, they threw him in the slammer for four days' solitary confinement, and doubled his meds. Many a lonely night, listening to Ravi's nightmares and Ratso's snoring, I thought about Tony Trevino and his reckless bid for freedom.

There was more good news. Although the gym felt like one big jail cell, most PE went on out of doors, even in winter, where in spite of the bitter cold I was relieved to be out beneath the open sky.

On the downside, the daily drug regime depressed me physically and mentally; lessons six mornings a week were dire: no music, no arts and crafts or science experiments – just literacy, numeracy and facts. And monthly sessions with a psychologist colleague of Dr Doughnut that did my head in. She made it her mission to cure me of my closed-door phobia by keeping the door closed, and probing me with questions designed to prove my aversion was a dodge to avoid school.

Monthly family visits – Sundays only – had to be earned by good behaviour. Most slogs were allowed out for lunch, four-hour *exeats* which took in the tea house in Skome, forty-nine miles away. Most families opted for a picnic in the great hall, or in the rose garden if the weather was fine. My mum or dad and sister Clem came every month without fail by tube, train and taxi, getting up at 5 a.m. to make it.

There were about sixty slogs in Dovedale when I was there, divided into three year-groups. Our days were regimented from beginning to end. Breakfast started at 7 a.m. sharp. Or to be precise, slogs had to have both feet in the dining hall by seven in order to join the dope queue. When the last boy was dosed up on Kalmasol-this or Kalmasol-that, breakfast began with Grace, led by a trusty toff in a fake solemn tone, like a serial killer reading a bedtime story. Ravi was Hindu and there was at least one Muslim in the joint, but Christianity was the only religion on the menu.

After breakfast, teeth-brushing and run, we returned to the coop, where we had thirty minutes to tidy our personal area and get to lessons by eight-thirty. A slog's personal area was defined by a box painted on the floor with white lines. Inside the box was an iron bed, chair and a chest of drawers. If you had any sense, you put a lot of care into making your bed, with the bottom sheet tucked in regulation-wise, top sheet smoothly turned over and pillow laid out straight. Pyjamas had to be precisely folded and slid under the pillow so you couldn't see them. One false crease or a hint of jim-jam showing, and Mr Strang or Mr Trust stripped the bed and made you start again. The only difference was old Moses sighed as he did it, like, 'Not good enough, son,' or, 'This won't get you to the promised land,' and might even leave your bottom sheet in place – whereas old Strang took pleasure in dragging everything off and dumping it on the deck. He once made Ratso remake his bed seventeen times, a Dovedale record of which Ratso was terrifically proud.

Your regulation tweedy slippers had to be placed exactly together and straight, toes touching the white line. Your chair had to be bare, except for your uniform overnight. Nothing was to spoil the shiny top of your chest of drawers. In the top right-hand drawer, along with a compulsory Bible – an inscribed gift from the Iceberg – you were allowed a small picture frame holding one family photo. In the left-hand drawer, one *approved* work of non-fiction, as well as a pad of writing paper, packet of envelopes and biros.

In your middle drawer you kept vests and underpants exactly folded, as well as socks rolled and neatly stacked. In the bottom drawer you kept your spare orange tracksuit and three sky-blue T-shirts, all perfectly folded. Every item had to have your name and number sewn in. Just as well Dovetail did that for us, because I'd never learned to sew, and Mum could never replace a shirt button without stabbing herself and reaching for the gin. Except for trainers, which were kept in the gym, footwear with laces was not permitted. Nor was any string allowed – no school tie, or anything that might be used to do yourself in. Even bedding and curtains were made of some shred-resistant material to deter hanging.

A typical weekday looked like this:

6.30: Up and wash.

7.00: Dope and breakfast.

7.30: Run.

8.00: Tidying personal area.

8.30–13.00: Lessons, with a thirty-minute break at ten-thirty.

13.00: Lunch.

14.00–17.00: PE and sport, shower.

17.30: Tea.

18.00–19.30: Homework in the 'den'.

19.30–20.30: Reading, reflection, letters home.

20.30: Wash and bed, quiet time.

21.00: Lights out.

Sunday mornings were different: the day began an hour later, and lessons were replaced by a two-hour assembly with hymn singing in the great hall – a huge room hung with shields and lances and paintings of men hunting and posh ladies posing with lapdogs. Stags' heads with massive antlers looked dumbly down from the walls. A female flying vicar led a religious service alongside the Iceberg. There was a lectern, an improvised altar with flowers and a crucified Jesus gazing sadly down on us like a former Dovedale slog. If they'd had Kalmasol in his day, he'd have been on it for sure. Dovedale's choir, coached by the Rev, had seven boys in it, including Shelly and Ravi, despite Ravi being a Hindu. 'Long as you sing with feeling,' she told him, 'I don't mind if you're a Martian.' The Iceberg's speciality was to read a passage from the Bible and weave in an up-to-the-minute message about some billionaire who gave everything to the poor, or some washed-up rock star who found Jesus and shot back up the charts.

Sunday afternoons were the same as weekdays – PE and sport, unless you had a family visit.

There wasn't much time to think, yet I thought of nothing but escape. Lying in bed at night, sloping along icy corridors, looking up from my classwork or jogging round the rugby pitch, always the same tension, the same thoughts filtering through the Kalmasol screen: How to get out of here and when to make my move? I wasn't fit enough yet, my body was still resisting the drugs. I was afraid I'd break out one night full of fire, run out of fuel and get recaptured like Tony Trevino. They'd pin another six months on my sentence and I'd go round the twist. I even began to wonder, against my deeper instincts, whether it wouldn't be better to try and stick it out for six months and get released, as promised, for good behaviour.

Boys who make good progress are generally released after six.

And then I thought, You must be joking!

My coopmates were nervous of me at first – and I of them. I thought they were all nuts, but soon began to realize they were just unlucky. The eldest was Sheldon

Barnicote, or Shelly. Whips and slogs called him Petticoat. He'd already done six weeks in Dovedale by the time I arrived. He was in for persistent cross-dressing, and violence when challenged. He was a tall Welsh lad with a manly voice, who kept a secret stash of lipstick and nail polish under a floorboard, and occasionally paraded at night in a bath towel as a dress. He came from a good home – private schools, *Sunday Times*, Golden Retriever. But listen closer and you learned that Shelly had a chronic smother-mother and a violent RAF officer dad. Catching his only son dressed as a girl used to make Dad Barnicote go ballistic. They were only too relieved that Sheldon was in Dovedale getting help for his condition, trusting the meds and discipline would make him normal. 'But what's *normal*, for God's sake?' Shelly complained. 'Parading in fancy dress and bombing people in faraway countries like my dad? Beating up his own son?'

Aside from dressing up as a girl, Shelly was like anybody else. The few minutes of free time we got, he listened to the Red Hot Chili Peppers and dreamed of being a rock star. He was cool most of the time, but you wanted to watch your tongue. Ratso – a seasoned street fighter – called him a perv once and got smacked around the room. Shelly told me how he once flipped and cracked his dad over the head with a cricket bat. You had to laugh: Air Commodore Barnicote – decorated for heroics in Iraq – comes home and cops it from his own son! Shelly was on Kalmasol-M, same as me – M for medium strength. It generally made him quiet and withdrawn. Some days he wasn't really there at all.

Then there was His Majesty Ravi Sharma, who'd only been in Dovedale a couple of weeks when I arrived. He was born in Bolton, parents from Madras. Old Ravi was nearly too wide for the toilet cubicles. When he walked, his flesh lumbered along trying to keep up. He was obsessed with food and ate like a starved dog. Sometimes the portions at supper were measly and he'd panic, and we'd slip him a few extra chips to calm him down. He joked and laughed, but you knew he was unhappy. He was in for good old ADHD as well as persistent delinquent behaviour – tickling people, hugging strangers, bullying little kids out of lunch boxes. His speciality was flashing his enormous bum – out of the window at his last school; out of the courtroom window! That's why the nickname, Flasher. Apparently his mum was an independent sort and didn't kowtow to mother-in-law, so his dad and uncles battered her. When she still wouldn't toe the line, they threw her out. Ravi had nightmares about it, called out for his mum in his sleep. He was also a flipping genius. Under the guidance of his granddad he'd passed an A level in Computer Science at the age of nine! Poor old Ravi. Who wouldn't be hyperactive, delinquent and asthmatic after they'd kicked out your mum and hothoused your brain till it smoked?

Ravi was prey to depression, but also had a knack of

jogging us out of ours. Cloaked in a bed sheet and wearing an improvised crown, he went round with his nose in the air saying, 'Get out of my sight, you *peasants*!' Or, 'I really can't believe I'm confined with such appalling *riffraff*.' He daydreamed of being a rich boss one day, fussed over by a gaggle of accountants, lawyers and chefs. He was on Kalmasol-M, plus the even heavier Kalmasol-X, which made him puke a lot, but we won't go into that. Even drugged out of his head he was nuts – in a nice kind of way, like an overgrown pup off its chain. He farted like a gong during lessons. *CWD – Compulsive Wind Disorder.*

And there was Ratso – real name Archie Manzini. He'd already done six months, and with no possibility of early release, was starting another six. It was hard work liking old Archie. He came from a desperately deprived family, and cancer killed his mum when he was a kid. He didn't know where he was born and wasn't a hundred per cent sure when. His dad had washed his hands of him and Archie was parcelled from one foster family to another, dragging a tank of stick insects with him. He was in Dovedale for persistent thieving and threatening behaviour, not to mention trying to set fire to his school – and to himself. He was missing half a thumb after a firework accident, but it didn't stop him being a slick-fingered pickpocket. Like Ravi, he was on Kalmasol-M and X. They once put him on XL4, the strongest brew of all, and he went mega-paranoid and thought we were all out to kill him. Actually, maybe that *wasn't* paranoia.

Archie acted like a cornered rat. Hated the world and everyone in it. They say he terrorized his last foster family into buying him flashy trainers and paying his mobile phone bills. He was barely literate and thought the Union Jack was a pop group, Mount Everest a race-horse and that psychopaths were reserved for bicycles. If you laughed, you were liable to have pepper flung in your eyes, or your locker set on fire. If anything went missing from your locker, it was always Archie, unless it was edible, and then it was Ravi. Archie also had the irritating habit of cracking his fingerbones, which drove everyone round the twist. *CBD – Compulsive Bone-cracking Disorder.*

Life in the coop was grim at first. The daily drugs that were supposed to keep us calm seemed to create a mood of edgy paranoia. Shelly kept himself to himself, while Ravi and Ratso never tired of trying to needle each other when whips were out of earshot.

'Get back to Pakiland, you big fat lump!'

'*Lump? Fat? Big?* I'm living with a Classics scholar!'

'We Brits are too soft – I'd put you all on the first boat.'

'My dear Ratso, I hail from the red rose county of Lancashire, and my ancestors were aristocrats from *India*, not Pakistan, you ignoramus.'

'What's the difference? You're still a Paki.'

47

'Really?' Ravi mocked him. 'And were I to lose my rag and tear you limb from limb, and were you rushed to casualty only to find the resident surgeon was – God forbid! – a Paki—?'

'I'd rather die than let a Paki touch me!'

Ravi could only laugh. 'How privileged one is to share accommodation with such a refined sage.'

Tired of trying to provoke Ravi, Ratso set his sights on me. I hated the whole sorry business, but just smiled, which got right up his nose. Sundays 6–8 p.m. we were allowed to watch telly and cook for ourselves in the den we shared with four other slogs, and one evening I was rustling up a risotto when Ratso took exception to the foreign stink and opened a window; when I didn't react, he grabbed the pan and emptied my entire meal in the bin. I felt like emptying him in the bin, but I don't do violence, unless strictly necessary – like if a mate's being attacked, or an old person, or the time I caught kids setting light to a kitten. But Ratso dumping my dinner? Nah! It was only out of a packet anyway and was frankly revolting.

'So what you gonna do about it, eh, Noodle Head?' said Ratso, parading the pan.

Shelly, Ravi and the others stopped to watch. Me, I started rapping:

> *'Cool it, Mr Ratso,*
> *You doing me a favour,*

> *You didn't like the aroma,*
> *I didn't dig the flavour . . .'*

'You're weird, you are!' Ratso jeered.

> *'All this packet racket*
> *Is making me lazy,*
> *The Es in my veins*
> *Are driving me crazy!'*

'Laugh all you like,' he told me, 'but what you gonna do while we're all eating our supper, eh? You tell me that.'

For reply I plucked a tin of beans from my locker, tossed it over my head, caught it behind my back and smiled at him. I was hoping that'd put a lid on it, but he wasn't finished – he went for my locker and dragged half the contents onto the floor – school books, pens and Bob Marley mug, which shattered in a thousand pieces – and looked at me like, *Now what ya gonna do?*

He wanted blood – he was twirling the frying pan in his fist, a lightweight aluminium number, but handy enough. I looked down at my Bob Marley mug scattered everywhere, turned to my locker and in a one sweep emptied the rest of it on the floor. I stepped up to him, eyeball to eyeball.

'You trying to chisel me, boss?' I said. 'You'll have to do better than that.'

Staring wildly at me, he flung the pan at the wall and stormed out.

Man, it was war! We were all shook up and lonely and took it out on each other. Nowhere was safe those first few bone-chilling weeks. The whole place ran on fear, like a bonfire on scrap and old tyres, and we were the scrap and tyres. Still, you make your choices. You allow yourself to get squashed or you don't. You stay scared out of your wits, or you say, *No! I'm not having it.* You go round cagey and twitchy and attracting the likes of Vinny Litner and Strangeboy Bland, or you lift your head and look them in the eye. It doesn't always work, but you feel better.

I tried to resist the climate of fear, went around alert, but with a ready smile, especially for my coopmates. I suggested a 50p fine for anyone using a cruel nickname, and started calling Ratso by his real name, Archie, and Flasher, Ravi, Shelly, Sheldon. This didn't trigger wild applause. Archie objected to being called Archie, on account of who the hell was I to call him by his name? Only friends were allowed to do that, and he didn't have any! And Shelly hated his real name, and called *himself* Shelly, so I said fine. Ravi pretended otherwise, but soon confessed he'd like to be called by his real name. A few weeks of me staying cool and refusing to get in on the negatives, and my coopmates began to loosen up. They, who trusted no one, began to drop their shoulders and share a laugh. Instead of us four hurting each other, we began to close ranks. Bit by bit, the tone in our alley changed.

I still couldn't decide whether to try and escape, or knuckle down. A month went by, two. It began to look like madness planning a breakout with nine weeks done and fifteen to go. My head said *Wait*, my heart said *Run*.

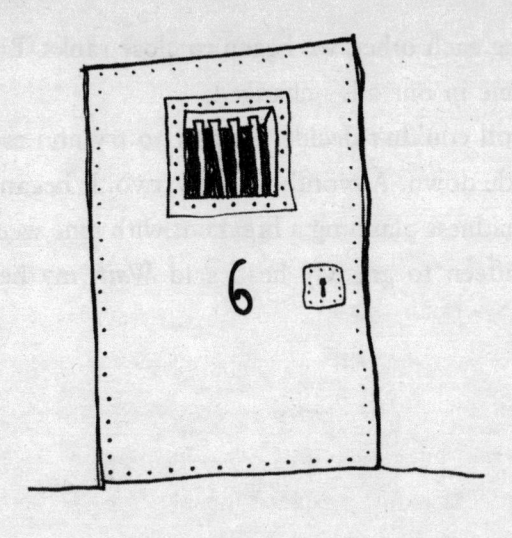

Crocuses poked through the icy crust, the snows retreated, the wind rattling the windows lost its bite. I grew used to captivity, whips yelling at me, slogs giving me grief, brutal fortnightly haircuts. It was nothing to be spat on, racially taunted, robbed at the point of a homemade knife. Nasty was normal – but I refused to be provoked, because I'd stopped flip-flopping between running or not running, I'd made my decision to stick it out, and started counting down the days to my release.

I hated my decision because I hated captivity, but I wasn't as desperate as some. Dezzie Phelps, a supposedly cool drug-dealer from Hull, couldn't hack the time and tried to top himself in May in a coop on the next floor. We woke up in the night to hear the whole grisly business: Moses found him just in time to cut him down, groaning, 'Holy Jesus, what in the world . . . ? Get back to bed all of you – now!'

Some lads turned to God out of sheer friggin' desperation. Me, I nearly got religion out of sheer flippin' gratitude the day our regular teacher left, and someone made a mistake and replaced him with an angel called Alison Cumberland – or Alice in Wonderland, as we called her. Maybe it was hard finding anyone willing to live and work in Dovedale, or maybe she said the right things about drugs and discipline at the interview.

Alice became our teacher and personal tutor. She had a soft spot for each of us, even Archie. She was a funny shape, like God had put her together out of off-cuts at the end of a roll, and she was kind of busty, which was nice. When you're facing into a long sentence and haven't seen or touched a girl for a hundred years, it felt wonderful – felt human – to look up from your work and see a really nice woman; not as sexy as the Iceberg, but a lot more attractive. Her hair was a bit of a calamity, but she wore bright dresses and had lovely eyes, and when she smiled she looked quite pretty. No question, we loved her.

She believed in us, said things like, 'You can manage your own behaviour, I know you can.'

'Without drugs?' I asked.

She hesitated. I pressed her.

'Level with us, miss – do we need medicating?'

'I think most of you need help, Marcus.'

'That's not what I asked.'

'I believe in free will,' she said carefully, 'and that you boys are capable of taking responsibility for your own actions without the need for drugs – but don't quote me.'

'My dear Miss Cumberland,' Ravi piped up, 'your sentiments move me, but I have to tell you, you haven't seen me without my Kalmasol – or half the lunatics in this establishment.'

'Sorry, Rav, I don't agree,' I said. 'Whatever's tormenting us, drugs'll only push it down and make it worse.'

'What do you know, Marcus?' said Shelly. 'Are you medically qualified?'

'What do doctors know?' I argued back.

'Ah, c'mon.'

'Just 'cos the dope's prescribed by someone in a white coat—'

'Yes – with years of training.'

'They're still only licensed drug-dealers.'

'Leave it out, Marcus, you're only trying to wind us up.'

'Just say no,' I smiled, 'that's what I say!'

'Who gives a monkey's,' said Archie, 'so long as you get a buzz?'

'Some of us *need* them, Marcus,' Shelly snapped. 'How else do you survive in a hole like this?'

'By resisting,' I said, 'in whatever way you can, big

or small, before they turn us into zombies. I mean, do any of you ever stop to think about the long-term effects of this stuff? Not to mention going through merry hell trying to come off it?'

'Calm down, lads, calm down,' said Alice, looking on in shock and sympathy.

She had her hands full with us lot. There were eight of us in the class, we four and the four we shared a den with. They weren't quite as wild and screwy as us – they seemed to lack confidence and larked about like kids or drifted into silent stupors. But we four hung together and gave off energy no dope could totally smother. Archie was always trying to needle Alice, clicking his fingers, mumbling obscenities, putting slugs in her shoulder bag, but all she'd say was, 'Sorry, I didn't quite catch that, Archie,' or 'Hmm, I wonder where they came from?'

Ravi tested her by letting off an enormous fart in the middle of a lesson; he put his ear to his desk and said, 'Good Lord, nine point two on the Richter Scale!'

'That's quite a talent, Ravi – could you repeat that for us?'

It was my turn. One Monday morning, edgy and depressed, I said, 'Miss, your lessons are dire.'

'I'm sorry to hear that,' she smiled. 'I'll have to try harder in future.'

I tried harder. 'Miss, you're the most boring teacher I've ever had.'

I saw the pain in her eyes, and felt ashamed. She looked down at her desk, and seemed to gather herself to hit me with detention or a furious lecture. Instead, just as I was starting to apologize, she said, 'You're right. I *am* boring. But you know what, Marcus, I think *you* have the makings of a fine teacher. How about taking the rest of the lesson?'

Everyone laughed and looked at me. Good move, I had to admit.

'Sure, why not?' I said and wandered to the front, flicked a stick of chalk over my head and caught it behind my back. While Alice sat in my place, I puffed out my chest and took the class.

'Right, Ravi – what's two and two?'

'Five, sir.'

'Five? Hmm, close. Shelly, two and two?'

'Twenty-two, sir.'

'Interesting answer. Have you thought about a career in military intelligence?'

I kept a straight face, playing to Alice.

'Archie?' I continued.

'What?'

'What do you mean, *what*? The nation's shelling out a fortune sending you to this academy – least you can do is pay attention. Now answer the question.'

'What question?'

'What's two plus two?'

'I dunno – a boy band?'

'Yo! Archie, top of the class! And I tell you what, as you've all been so good, I'm gonna give you the rest of the lesson off. Draw, play cards, do what you like!'

Everyone laughed – all except Alice, who sat observing while I leaned back in her chair, hands behind my head. And then, just as we were beginning to tire of lounging around, someone said, 'Ah, sir, I'm bored out of me flippin' skull. Teach us something, for God's sake!'

Who was that? *Miss!* Everyone laughed!

'Oi, you lot, shuddup,' she said, 'or I'll smash yer faces in!'

'Quiet, all of you!' I said, finding my teacher's voice. 'And as for you' – pointing at Alice – 'any more threats of violence—'

'Bog off, sir!'

Everyone choked.

'What did you say, boy?' I said.

'You're the most boring, snot-faced teacher I've ever known. Get off me back or I'll slash yer tyres.'

The class erupted.

'Right, Mr King,' I said, 'you're going straight to Mr Strang.'

'Make me.'

I couldn't believe her cheek!

'Watch me!' I said, coming down the room and freezing – because I obviously wasn't going to lay a hand on her.

She saw my problem, looked up and cried, 'It's him! He's coming!'

Everyone froze.

'Relax, no one's really coming,' she said in her own voice. 'Who wants to play Mr Strang? Winston? Donny?' She offered it to some of the others. 'Archie?'

'No way.'

'Shelly?' He shook his head.

Alice looked at Ravi.

'I thought you'd never ask,' he said, and got up and walked out.

And came back in again, flinging the door open.

'Marcus King, where is he?'

We gasped – the chilling resemblance to the Deputy Director.

'Who's been cheeking the teacher?' said Ravi, bearing down on Alice.

'Wasn't me, sir!' she protested.

'It never is, is it, boy?'

'It was them!' she cried, pointing at us. 'I was doing me work.'

'How fascinating. If there was a prize for mendacity, Mr King, you'd win it annually!' said Ravi, who then turned to me and said, 'Well, Miss Slumberland, what have you to say?'

Hoots of laughter.

'Marcus called me something shocking, sir,' I said miserably.

'What did he say? Speak up.'

'It's . . . it's too awful, Mr Strang.'

'Don't be ridiculous, woman. Speak or be sacked!'

'Marcus said I was a boring teacher!' I sobbed.

'Well, I suppose he has a point there,' said Ravi.

'He told me to bog off!'

'Ah well, that's perfectly reasonable.'

'And threatened to slash my tyres!'

'Oh, really! You teachers do nothing but fuss-fuss-fuss. If I had my way I'd sack the lot of you, and teach the brats myself! What *does* concern me is the state of this loathsome creature's uniform!' said Ravi, standing over Alice. 'In all my born days I have never encountered such a scruffy individual!'

The class nearly died. Alice looked gutted.

'Ah, sir, I do me best.'

'Your *best*?' said Ravi. 'Look at you, boy, coming to school in your mother's *dress*! And those earrings and nail polish are *strictly* against the rules. I'm frankly appalled,' he went on, mopping his brow. 'I've a good mind to retire to the country and race snails.'

'Punish her!' demanded Archie.

'*Him*, you fool! And who spoke out of turn?' boomed Ravi. 'A million lines! Now, where was I?'

'Keep it brief, sir,' said Alice. 'You're giving me a headache.'

'*What!* How dare you! It's high time I taught you a lesson, Mr King!' raved Ravi, snatching a ruler from

Alice's desk. 'Hold out your hand, boy.'

'Ah, sir . . .' Alice pleaded.

'Never mind *ah, sir*. Do it!'

Alice put out a hand. Ravi turned to us and said, 'Naturally, this is going to hurt me far more than it's going to hurt her— I mean *him*.'

'Please, sir, it could set off one of me epileptic fits.'

'I don't care if it sets off an epidemic of figs! I like beating boys. It's the only thing that gets me up in the morning.'

'Ah, sir, it's not fair.'

'*Fair?* What's fair got to do with it? You're a disgrace to your mixed race, Mr King, and I intend to reform you if it's the last thing I do.'

Alice extended a trembling hand – Ravi grabbed her fingertips, lifted the ruler and brought it down with a loud whack on the desk.

'*Ow!*'

Ravi grabbed her hand again and *whack!*

'*OW!*'

He was about to strike a third time when the door flew open. Mr Strang! Eyes blazing – 'What on earth . . . ?'

Everyone stunned.

'Is there no member of staff in here?'

Alice raised a hand.

'Miss Cumberland – what is going on?'

'We were doing some drama.'

'*Drama?* Don't you think we have enough drama in Dovedale, Miss Cumberland?'

'It was a role-reversal exercise . . .' Alice began to explain.

'Does Miss Rice-Bird know you're doing drama with these boys?'

'It happened spontaneously, as the best drama often—'

'Back to your places,' he ordered. 'Get out your books.'

'Excuse me, sir, which ones?' said Shelly.

'What day is it, Barnicote?'

'Monday, sir.'

'What time is it?'

Shelly looked at the clock. 'Five to nine, sir.'

'What books then?'

'Maths, sir.'

'Get on with your maths – and let's hear no more about drama.'

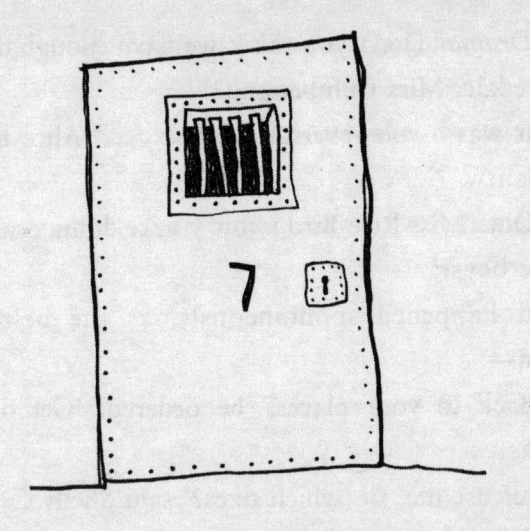

Summer arrived. After a nervy start back in January, I'd set out to be a model slog and I believed the whips were secretly impressed. The Iceberg was too busy to see me, but Mr Strang emerged from a staff meeting towards the end of June and instructed Clarence Trust to inform me that one more trouble-free month and my case would be reviewed, with every possibility of a positive outcome.

Brilliant! Curbing my instincts to run had paid off.

My coopmates were given no such good news, which meant that each of them would almost certainly have to do his full twelve-month stint. I felt sorry for them, but not sorry enough to want to join them.

I phoned home, told my delighted parents that, all being well, I'd be out in four weeks.

I continued to steer clear of trouble, worked hard, kept my bed area tidy and obediently swallowed my daily dope – though I hated doing it, hated that hollowed-out feeling, that sense of being at one remove from myself – anything to prove I was a reformed character. The days ticked by. I got more and more excited – thoughts of making my own music again, seeing family every day instead of every month, checking out mates and having a sixteenth birthday bash.

July 31st finally arrived – the big day. Case review with the Iceberg and the Predator at 5.45 p.m.

I was so jizzed up I woke before the alarm and looked out the window. A bright new day. I'm going south – I'm going home! A heatwave had hit the whole country. The fields and scrubland beyond the rose garden had flared into a riot of wild flowers. Swallows dipped and swooped above the trees, and at night you could see bats hunting along the edge of the wood, occasionally hear a spooky owl.

Now that I was leaving, the views from my window seemed more gripping than ever, and I tried to memorize every detail – the crumbling garden wall, shot with tiny blooms; the cracked and dried-up ornamental fountain; the edible parasol mushrooms and the giant cedar tree at the entrance to Strapps Wood.

Long as I didn't screw up today, I'd be jiving out that gate any time.

'Yo! Marcus, you're getting out of here!' I yelled at the mirror.

'Don't be so sure,' said Shelly.

'Why not? They more or less said one more month.'

'Never trust anyone.'

With morning lessons out the way, there was only one hurdle left to leap, the monthly Hare and Hounds, always a bit tense. Today was worse because it was the turn of our coop to be the hares. But nothing was going to side-track me – not today! I ignored the sulks of coopmates and classmates who weren't so thrilled I was leaving, and the taunts of enemies itching for a last go at me.

Every slog in Dovedale participated in the Hare and Hounds. It was the hares' job to shoot off across coun-try, leaving clues for the hunting pack of hounds – about fifty-five slogs strong – to follow. Any hare who made it back to Dovedale without being caught was a merry bunny, rewarded with a leisurely bath and a Mars Bar. But even with a five-minute start, we were running against slogs a year or two older than us, and the chances of getting overtaken and roughed up were excel-lent. Hounds that caught hares were rewarded with a bath, a Mars Bar and a crisp new fiver. The last ten hounds to finish were made to do a dozen circuits of Harry Headcase's gruelling assault course in the gym – not a lot of fun after a seven-mile marathon. Hares or hounds caught cheating were dispatched directly to the slammer.

The hounds naturally included Skinny Hitler and Strangeboy Bland, thugs who still starred in my nightmares. It was a source of nagging regret that I'd never managed to inflict on them the revenge I'd promised – I'd concentrated on keeping out of their way – but I wasn't planning to go looking for an opportunity today.

Harry Headcase handed out four yellow high-viz vests to us hares, and orange ones to the hounds. Then he checked his watch and grabbed Ravi's arm. The heat was fierce; Ravi's eyes swam with fear. He was a brain box, not built for out-running a pack of salivating hoodlums. He'd scarcely ever run a Hare and Hounds, always managing to pull an asthma attack out of the hat in the nick of time.

'I'm feeling good today, Michelin Man,' said Harry. 'I'm giving you a ten-minute start instead of the traditional five. What do you say to that?'

'You're a gentleman, sir!' said Ravi, close to tears.

'You don't look happy, boy – I can't understand it.'

'I'm so happy, sir, I could cry.'

'Pace yourself and you never know, all that surplus flesh might spontaneously convert to natural gas.'

The hounds split their sides.

'Flasher's gonna blow up today, sir!' predicted Skinny Hitler.

'Concentrate on *your* performance, lads. None of you managed to catch Petticoat last time, did you?'

They leered at Shelly. It really got up their noses that a boy who dressed like a girl could run like the wind.

Harry Headcase dished out the blackboard chalk. Every hundred metres or so, the hares were supposed to chalk an arrow on a tree or rock to show which way they'd gone. When the hounds were released, they followed the arrows. Harry tossed a green stick of chalk to Shelly, blue to Archie and red to me. Finally he slapped a white piece into Ravi's sweaty palm.

'Right, Mr Sharma, Olympic glory beckons! Three, two, one – you're off!'

We watched Ravi blunder away like a startled walrus. Hounds laughed and rubbed their hands.

Skinny Hitler and Strangeboy Bland turned their attention to me, no doubt recalling my first Hare and Hounds back in early Feb, when I mistook five minutes for a handy start, and was amazed how fast they and others ran me down and beat me up. They grinned at me behind Sir's back, grinding fists into palms, drawing fingers across throats. I returned their gazes, reminding myself that very soon, while these clowns were playing Al Capone in Dovedale, I'd be hanging out with mates, taking a girl to a movie or sunning myself on my nana's fire escape down at the Oval, watching the cricket through binoculars.

Five minutes after Ravi's release, Harry Headcase placed a hand on Archie's shoulder. 'Are we ready, Ratso? England expects!'

To jeers from gleeful hounds, Archie shambled off, half running, playing it cool. My turn next.

I'll never forget that day! It was hot as hell, but who cared? I'd done my stint. *This is it!* I kept telling myself. *I'm getting out of here!*

Harry's hand was on my shoulder. My heart beat wildly. I could feel the pent-up energy of fifty-odd slogs behind me.

'Destiny calls, Noodle Head! Three, two, one . . .'

I was away, running on shaky legs, the heat intense, cool woods calling. Behind me I could hear Shelly being released. A shadow caught mine and he passed me, flinging me an anxious smile. I tried to stay with him, but he had limbs of fire. For a time I caught snatches of his yellow vest way ahead. Then there was nothing of him left but green arrows scrawled on tree trunks – and I was alone in the woods with broken sunlight and scraps of sky. Now and then a hastily scratched white or blue arrow gave off silent echoes of Ravi and Archie.

I was running smoothly, cool but not complacent. Any second now, Sir would fire a starting pistol to signal the hounds were off. I stopped to chalk up another red arrow and kept going, wondering where the hell everyone had got to.

What a day! Goodbye, Dovedale! *Adios amigos!*

The woods closed in like walls; sweat streamed in my eyes.

Bang!

That's it, they're off! C'mon, Marcus – lift off! Pump blood!

Fear and determination can you make you run like hell, and I ran like hell that day. The meds slowed me down a bit, but my body was used to them, and the hounds were all Kalmasoled too.

Then – someone ahead on my path! For a terrible moment, I thought it was Skinny Hitler. But it was only Archie, leaning on a tree – smoking a cig, for crying out loud, not a care in the world.

'Archie, what's the story?'

'Taking it easy – what do you think?'

'Sure, what's the rush?' I said, rolling my eyes.

'What's the rush? You mad?' he cried. 'They're gonna *kill* me. Do me a favour, will ya?' he said, holding out his chalk.

'You gotta be joking,' I said, running on.

'Oh, thanks a million!' he called. 'Have a nice life.'

I hesitated – he pleaded, 'Please, Marco, I'll make it up to ya! I'll rob a bank and split it with you when I get out! I'll lend you me Roller – *please*!'

'Quick!' I called.

He flung me his chalk and a fiendish grin, tore off his yellow vest and scuttled into the trees, leaving me to lay a false trail for him so he could cut back home to an early bath, swearing blind he'd got clean away. I ran on, trying to pick the quickest paths through the trees, leaping puddles and ditches, marking up blue and red arrows as I went.

Behind me the sound of baying and barking came

in waves through the trees, Skinny and his hounds trying to make us even more frightened than we already were.

Come on, come on! Faster now, faster, pausing only to gulp great mouthfuls of air and chalk another red arrow, another blue one. Trodden paths led deeper into the woods. Soon the trees would peter out and I'd break into open moorland and catch sight of Shelly heading for Fox Rock. Once you reached the rock, you had to scratch your initials as proof of passage, and press on in a wide loop around Dunnock Wood and over Stippleborne Hill back to Dovedale. Archie was taking a big chance, because whips often lay in wait at the rock.

'*Ruh-ruh-ruh-ruh!*' went the hounds, three or four minutes behind.

Stretch the pace, man – nice and smooth – that's it! I told myself, confident that I had plenty left in reserve. Wo! Who's that ahead – slumped against a tree?

'Hey, Ravi! Taking five?'

Help me! his face was saying.

'Come on, Rav – get up!'

I can't, his eyes replied. *I've had it!*

'They'll waste you, Rav, c'mon!' I said, trying to lift a mountain.

'*Ruh-ruh-ruh-ruh!*'

As I glanced back, Ravi stared at the two chalks in my hand, and his stricken face said, *Hey, what about me?*

'Godsake!' I said, grabbed his white chalk and drew a white arrow pointing straight ahead. 'Pick a spot, Rav, and stay down!'

Struggling to his feet, he stumbled away, giggling helplessly.

I ran on, carrying three bits of chalk, red, white and blue – *God Save the Queen!* – and, glancing back, saw Ravi tearing off his vest and descending into undergrowth like a hippo into water. Then in the distance I caught flashes of vivid orange swarming through the trees – a minute away – and took off like a deer from a forest fire. But it was no good, my legs weren't responding; I'd underestimated the Kalmasol and was running out of juice.

Do something!

I'd read about exhausted foxes fooling a pursuing pack by turning back towards it, and the hounds, noses to the ground and not expecting it, completely miss the fox sauntering by the other way. These dogs would never fall for that, but I had think of something and all I could think of was *Up!* Casting around for a tree with manageable branches, I chalked one last red arrow, one white and one blue, all pointing straight ahead, and shinned up a tree, melting into foliage.

Squinting back the way I'd come, I could just make out the first hounds pausing on the track where I'd left Ravi. Moments later, they came bursting into view – paused to take in my last three arrows and dashed on, followed by dozens more hounds strung out through the trees in threes and fours. The baying and roaring faded, the woods fell still.

I held my breath – something was wrong. Unless they'd gone another way, or I'd somehow missed them, two crucial hounds were missing. Wait a second – here they come, Skinny Hitler and Strangeboy Bland, not even running – strolling into the clearing, swinging sticks like idle golfers, chatting and whistling. What a life! Strangeboy having a lazy stretch, Skinny Hitler perching on a stump to roll a joint. A joint! Where had he got that from? We'd all been had. Those threats behind Sir's back! They'd planned this little caper. They'd have their smoke and go home, accusing us cheats of leading them astray. Skinny started practising golf swings with his stick, dreaming of famous fairways. Strangeboy stretched out on the ground, taking slow pulls on the joint like a gangster planning his next operation.

Smoke curled itself around a sunbeam.

Now what? Skinny Hitler was pricking his ears – he'd heard something. He was whispering to Strangeboy and they were turning back – stealthily. Suddenly I knew what it was. A shout! More shouts. A struggle in the trees and then, as I feared, Ravi came storming out of the undergrowth like a maddened buffalo with two lions on his back. Leaning out of my tree, I could see the fear in his face as he tried to escape. He was putting up a struggle, but soon as he flung them off, they were all over him again, tripping him, dragging him down.

Laughing hysterically, they sat on him, bouncing up and down. One of the hounds is supposed to escort a captured hare back to Dovedale, while the others run on, but these slimeballs were having too much fun. Strangeboy dragged Ravi's tracksuit down, Skinny Hitler lifted his stick. Leaning further, I flinched at every blow as if it was me they were beating, praying that Harry Headcase was following up.

Seconds passed. *Do something, Marcus!*

No! Stay put. Don't get involved!

But the hitting didn't stop, and Harry Headcase didn't show, and I couldn't stand it. Next thing I know, I'm dropping to the ground, heart pounding – moving softly back to the clearing, where Ravi lay face down in the dust, Skinny's foot on his head while Strangeboy lashed his raw bum with spiky brambles, mocking him and calling him disgusting names.

'Afternoon, gentlemen! This looks fun – two against one.'

They looked round in surprise, and I should like to report that I used all my well-known wit and reasoning skills to persuade them to leave my friend alone, but instinct took over and I flung myself at them, lashed out with everything I had – fists, feet and fingernails. They could have skinned me alive, but I was too quick, too scared, and next thing I knew, Ravi was on his feet, mad as a wounded rhino. Grabbing Strangeboy from behind, he swung him round and round in a fit of rage and released him like a discus into the bushes, where Strangeboy smacked his head on a tree trunk – leaving me face to face with Skinny Hitler, coming at me teeth bared, hands balled into fists, and there's no doubt he would have murdered me had I not struck first like a snake, two stiff fingers in his assassin's eyes – *stab!* Once more for good measure – *stab!*

Skinny's scream ripped through the trees.

'Marcus – look out!'

Ravi's cry came too late to prevent Strangeboy grabbing me from behind. Wrestling me to the ground, he went to smash a fist in my face when again I struck first – seized his nuts.

The louder he yelped, the harder I squeezed.

'Geddoff!'

'Give in?'

'Lemme go!'

'I said, Give in?'

'Yes!'

'Good move, boss,' I said, and rolled away.

As Skinny Hitler's groans echoed on the breeze, Harry Headcase hobbled into the sunlight on his cane, and gaped at the sight of two senior slogs on their knees – Vinny Litner holding his face and Liam Bland cradling his nuts – and gazed at me and Ravi as we shrugged apologetically, like – *Oops! Did we overdo it?* But before Sir could finish spluttering, 'What the hell is going on

73

here?' Ravi collapsed and rolled in the dust, like someone had flicked a switch and put a million volts through him.

'Enough of your fakery, Sharma,' bellowed Sir. 'Get up!'

Ravi had gone the colour of mustard and was having an asthma attack, panic attack and possible heart attack rolled into one.

'I don't think he's messing, sir!' I cried. 'He needs help quick!'

Harry Headcase peered closer. Snapping out of his trance, he tossed me a phone and yelled me a number and lifted Ravi into a sitting position. Minutes later, a jeep smashed into the clearing, Moses at the wheel. Out bumbled Dr Doughnut – plunged a loaded syringe into Ravi's thigh.

We all got a ride home, where Ravi was rushed into Dovedale's medical wing, the san. A local nurse arrived to assist – a curtain was thrown round Ravi's bed. I sat in the waiting area facing Strangeboy and Skinny, nursing my own cuts and bruises. Skinny – blind in both eyes and wincing with pain – kept saying, 'Where's he now?' and Strangeboy answered, 'Right opposite – keep telling you.'

'Tell him he's dead meat!'

'You tell him.'

'You're dead meat, Noodle Head, you hear me?'

'I hear you, Vinny – I'm dead meat.'

Shock was in my voice – and in his. I looked Strangeboy in the eye – grinned at him. His evil little eyes stared back out of his zit-scarred face saying, *You've not heard the last of this.*

Listening to Ravi being hooked up to a drip and wired to hell, my first thought was, Hope to God he's not going to die, and my second, Hope to hell there isn't trouble over this, 'cos Rav's in no shape to testify.

Dr Doughnut emerged.

I jumped up. 'Is he going to be OK?'

'Yes, of course, nothing to worry about.'

Skinny Hitler was in too much pain to open his eyes for Doughnut to examine them. 'Tell me straight, Doc,' he whined. 'Am I gonna lose my sight?'

'Hardly.'

The retinas of both eyes were scratched. Doughnut gave him drops and eye patches, which he'd have to wear for forty-eight hours. I glanced at the clock. Five fifteen. My case review was in half an hour. Doughnut turned his attention to Strangeboy's cut head.

'I'll have to pass, Doc,' I said, and ran.

When I reached the coop, Shelly and Archie were getting dressed after their luxury bath.

'You made it!' I said, giving them the thumbs up.

'No sweat!' said Archie.

'What about you, Marcus?' said Shelly.

'I just bowled along singing a song, minding my own business.'

'That's not what we heard.'

'What did you hear?'

'You and Ravi attacked the hounds with sticks and rocks.'

I laughed. 'Yeah, right.'

'You laid in wait for them and pounced as they went by.'

'You believe that?'

'No. But *they* might.'

I showered and ran back to put on clean tackle. Checked myself in the mirror.

Relax, Marcus – everything's cool.

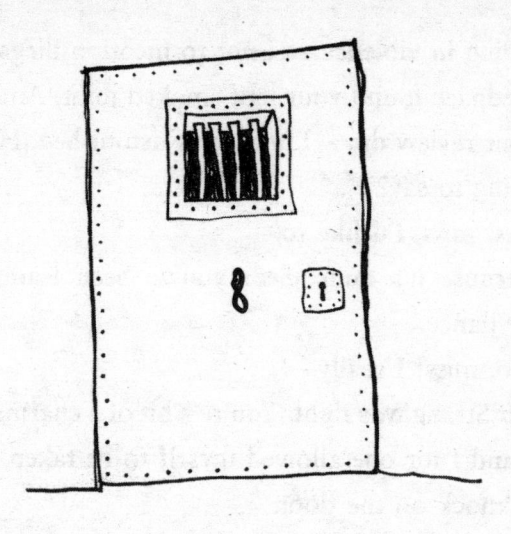

I presented myself outside the Iceberg's office at five forty-five on the nail. Took a deep breath and knocked. The Iceberg sat behind her desk, tapping a pen. She was all in pink, lips and fingernails to match.

On her right sat the Predator, arms folded.

'Stand up straight, boy,' he said.

I was standing straight, but reshuffled myself all the same.

The Iceberg gazed at me. 'I'm disappointed, Mr King.'

'Oh, you mean what happened in the—?'

'There I was, fondly imagining you were making efforts to reform, but evidently I was mistaken.'

'No, miss, you weren't—'

'Do you know what I've been doing all afternoon? Making the necessary arrangements to facilitate your return to society. And what have you been doing?

Indulging in violence . . . not to mention illegal drugs. Mr Ledpace found your half-smoked joint. And all this on your review day – I'm frankly astonished. Have you anything to say?'

'Yes, miss, I'd like to—'

'Because it's quite clear you've been leading us a merry dance.'

'No, miss! I really—'

'Mr Strang was right. You're a bit of a charmer, aren't you, and I for one allowed myself to be taken in.'

A knock on the door.

'Enter.'

In came Strangeboy Bland – head bandaged – leading Skinny Hitler by the arm. Blinded by eye patches, Skinny shuffled nervously forward, not trusting his pal, who'd probably steered him into doors all the way down.

'Well, gentlemen, would you care to repeat what you told Mr Ledpace?'

I knew from her tone that the word of Vinny Litner and Liam Bland – both Trusted Offenders – would carry more weight than mine or Ravi's.

'Well, miss, we were following the arrows, running hard – I mean, we're pretty good at Hare and Hounds,' said Skinny Hitler, 'when all of a sudden, these two jokers, King and Sharma, leap out the bushes swinging clubs and hurling rocks. Couldn't believe it. I mean, you don't expect that kind of thing – it's supposed to a sport – we never even got a chance to—'

'Thank you, Mr Litner. Mr Bland, is that your inter-pretation?'

'Except for one thing, miss,' declared honest Bland. 'We tried to reason with them – didn't we, Vinny? – make them see sense. But they were – I mean, *phew*' – he blew in total disbelief – 'totally out of control.'

I was looking at Strangeboy. He was looking away.

'Mr King?' The Iceberg cocked an eyebrow.

'I know it looks bad, miss, but—'

'Are you *that* fond of us? Can't you bear to be parted from Dovedale Hall? You realize you've put me in the unenviable position of having to explain these injuries to the boys' families? Not to mention the police – we're talking about a serious assault. Fortunately for you, I've Dovedale's reputation to consider and have decided to deal with it myself. I'll be speaking to your parents today. I feel extremely let down, as I'm sure they will.'

'I promise you, Ms Iceberg, you got it wrong . . . I've worked hard and steered clear of—'

The shock on their faces told me what I'd just called her.

'Sorry, miss, it just slipped out.'

'Watch your tongue!' roared Mr Strang.

From the Iceberg, a graceful sigh. 'Mr King, you clearly haven't reformed and I am postponing your release indefinitely. Expect to remain with us for at least another six months. After that, if your behaviour merits it, I may be willing to discuss it again. Take him away.'

Someone behind me – Harry Headcase – jerked my arm up behind my back – *Ow!* – and shoved me out the room and down the corridor.

'Take it easy, sir – there's no need for that.'

Across the entrance hall and past the dining hall he marched me, kicked open an old door and bundled me down a flight of stone steps to a musty underground passage, where a steel door opened into a high-ceilinged chamber.

'Go on – get in there.'

This was one of two legendary slammers – converted wine cellars, known officially as Solitary Reflection Units, where you were supposed to think about what you'd done and come to your senses. I stepped inside and turned round.

'I thought you were different,' said Harry, 'but you're just as feckless and shiftless as all the rest of these incorrigible wasters – am I right?'

'Yeah, you're right – that's all I am.'

With that he swung the door closed, locked it with a massive key, lashed home the bolts and walked away, cursing under his breath.

I stood gazing at the locked door. Panic slid its fingers round my throat.

You clearly haven't learned your lesson . . . I'm postponing your release indefinitely.

The cell was cool and unnaturally silent. The walls and floor were covered in dark-green rubber, like the mats you get in gyms, like a cave.

Expect to remain with us at least another six months.

Everything was green, still and silent.

At least another six months.

Worse right now, I was confined to a room with a closed and locked door. Panic gripped me – I shook it off. Self-pity moved in, I flung that off too. I wanted to sink to my knees, but stayed standing, not daring to move, not daring to feel.

Footsteps coming down the stairs. Keys jangled, the door opened. Mr Strang, suffering from hay fever, wiped his nose on an ample handkerchief and ducked into the cell. I returned his gaze. He put away the handkerchief and handed me a clipboard with a stack of A4 sheets attached, a biro and ruler.

'You're to write a full and frank apology to Miss Rice-Bird. If it isn't sufficiently sincere, if the handwriting isn't neat enough, if the date isn't clearly underlined, if it contains the smallest spelling mistake or grammatical error – if, in short, it isn't perfect, you'll remain here and keep revising it until it is. Do I make myself clear?'

I nodded. How much clearer could you get?

On his way out again he paused and turned.

'No supper, boy. Perhaps hunger will focus your mind on the required task.'

He went out, locking and bolting the door.

'Sir . . . Mr Strang, sir?' I called. 'Is it strictly necessary to lock the door?'

I heard him give a snort of derision, as though my enquiry wasn't worth the breath.

I stood holding the clipboard, pen and ruler. Slowly I turned and looked around. There was virtually nothing to break the cell's green embrace, only a high-up strip of window covered by a steel grille and open to let air in. With nothing to stand on, you couldn't look out, only up at a thin band of sky. Clouds hung in the blue. Out there was summer; in here was winter. I was incarcerated below ground, riding waves of panic. I kept wishing I had my pebbles with me – or even Email, my intrepid fighter-pilot mouse.

In one corner of the cell stood a plastic jug of water and a paper cup.

I slid to my knees in the middle of the floor, trying to work out what exactly had happened. My brain was scrambled, my mind blank. The terror could have been worse – the Kalmasol was dulling thoughts and feelings. But for throbbing bruises, I might have dreamed the incident in the woods. And to think that only a few hours ago I was all jizzed up with the promise of freedom. Then came baying hounds, Archie and Ravi begging for help, Skinny and Strangeboy smoking dope and spotting Ravi and then . . .

I really didn't want to think about it.

Silence.

Evening birdsong. Distant voices.

Expect to remain with us at least another six months.

It didn't sink in. How could it? I was nearly sixteen and mature, but that's all I was – nearly sixteen, cool on the outside but inside still a kid feeling his way, and all at once I ached for my mum's arms – longed for my dad to say, *It's OK, son, it wasn't your fault.*

Another six months.

I'd been due a visit from Mum and Dad – no chance of that now. They'd be very upset, and angry with me, believing that I'd gone and blown my release.

I wiped my eyes, placed the clipboard on the floor and lay down beside it, hands behind my head. Tried to keep my mind closed, let nothing in. I thought, If I can do that, if I can keep my mind closed, keep feelings outside the door, I can get through this without going crazy.

Trouble was, ten, fifteen minutes of solitary and you start going nuts. Twenty minutes or so passed – heavy footfalls. Someone coming down the stairs, stopping outside my cell – drawing back the spy hole. A pair of eyes looking in.

'Yo! Mr Trust, is that you?'

No reply.

'Mr Trust?'

The eyes stared in.

'Speak to me, will you?'

I remembered now – all part of the punishment, minimum communication with the prisoner.

'You'd do well to pray, boy.'

The spy hole closed, Moses left me.

'Hey, Mr Trust, what number's room service? Just getting a bit peckish . . . maybe a pizza, side salad, bottle of merlot . . .'

Silence. I was cold. My underground cell didn't know it was summer. I thought of the others having supper in the dining hall, my empty place. Hunger was feeding on my stomach. Worse was the feeling of being locked in. No – way – out. I'd go a week without food if they'd just open that door.

Man, this felt bad! I was jiggling with nerves – panicky like, *Oh Christ – I might just go crazy in here.* Felt like slamming my head against a wall, and remembered why the walls were padded with rubber.

I needed to take a leak. Got up and hammered on the door.

Sunset burned in the narrow window, but the cell was virtually dark. I kept hammering and yelling.

> *'Yo! Mr Jailer,*
> *I'm busting to go;*
> *Gonna flood the place*
> *If you don't show!'*

Someone coming down the stairs.

'Open up, will ya, boss!'

The spy hole shot open and a pair of eyes looked in.

'Man's gotta go when a man's gotta go – know what I mean?'

Moses escorted me in silence to the jacks, a cramped bog-and-basin conversion at the end of a spooky passage. Handed me my washbag, and waited, arms folded, while I brushed my teeth.

Glancing in the mirror, I caught his gaze. I wanted to talk about chess, boxing, the dynamics of paragliding – anything – but his empty gaze told me to zip it. When we got back to the slammer, someone had been in to unroll a thin mattress and leave two folded sheets, blankets and my pyjamas. You didn't get a pillow.

Moses looked at me. 'The help of God,' he growled, 'is nearer than the door.'

I frowned, like, *Thanks for that*. He locked me in and left.

'Mr Trust?' I called. 'I can't seem to find the TV guide or the remote. Oh, and maybe you could you send me over a couple more beers, and some crisps . . . maybe some olives . . . those soft sun-dried ones without the stones . . . Moroccan are best, in my experience . . .'

Mum loved olives. When friends came round she'd put out a selection of olives in a dish we'd brought back from Corfu. It was cracked and glued together, and had separate sections for black olives, green ones or those stuffed Italian ones. She served them with squares of feta cheese and chilled white wine. Mum had style. Missing her felt like a vice screwed tight around my heart. Worse was the thought of what she was going through, having to tell friends and relations that I'd done something shocking and my release had been cancelled.

The remaining light was being sucked out of the thin strip of window. The cell began to shrink. I'd have killed for my CD player. I made up the bed and got in and thought about Ravi in the san, and Shelly and Archie bedding down in the coop, talking about what had happened, or maybe not. It was hard having a conversation with Archie that didn't end with, *How the hell should I know?*

Darkness filled the cell to the brim. A nightlight glowed faintly above the door like an eye. I was wiped, but couldn't sleep.

Stars blinked in the window.

Three or four times an hour, old Moses flung back the spy hole, shone a torch in, shut the hole and went away again.

Six more months . . . swear to God I'll go crazy.

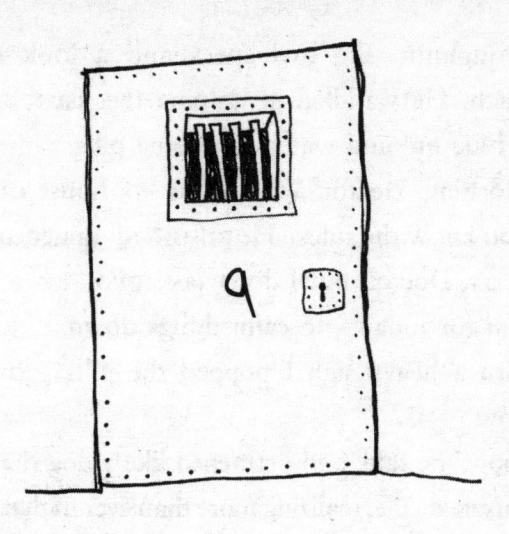

I woke to the six-thirty alarm going off way upstairs, realized where I was and still sat up, heart thumping, out of habit. And lay down again. One of the perks of the slammer – you don't have to break a leg every morning.

It was light, or as light as it gets in the eerie green cellar. Old Moses appeared and escorted me to the jacks.

'Morning, Mr Trust. What a party! I'm stiff from dancing. Hope the music didn't keep you awake.'

When I returned to the cell, my bed and bedding had been removed, no trace.

A little later, Moses pushed open my door and stood holding a breakfast tray, waiting for me to take it. I gazed at it, like I'd never seen a breakfast tray before. He put it down on the floor, and then I heard someone coming along the passage whistling a tune. Enter

Dr Doughnut. Big owl specs and a look of stern reproach. He waddled in holding the usual two little cups: blue pill and water. *Two* blue pills.

'Morning, Doctor. What's this – a house call?'

'You know the rules.' He tut-tutted, finger to his lips.

'Sorry, Doctor, but I don't take two.'

'Just for today – to calm things down.'

With a heavy sigh I popped the pills – but didn't swallow.

'Show,' he said, and I stiffened like a dog that doesn't want its medicine, realizing more than ever in that moment just how much I hated taking the stuff: the way it took hold of me, the way I had no choice – another no-way-out gig.

'Come along now, Malcolm, there's a good chap.'

I swallowed the pills, vowing that somehow I'd find a way of secretly not taking any more.

Dr Doughnut smiled and took himself off.

Moses locked me in and went off duty.

I looked down at my breakfast – a plastic bowl of milky cornflakes dusted with sugar, a paper cup of orange juice and a slice of white toast and marmalade. I picked up the tray and put it down in a corner – and turned my back on it.

Filled a cup with water and sipped it slowly.

My stomach growled, my head started to buzz, and kept buzzing through the long morning. My hands and legs soon got the shakes. Medication on an empty stomach's like a burning cigarette tossed in a waste-paper bin – I smouldered inside. I couldn't stop shaking. Every inch of flesh, every cell and muscle in my body was in motion, yet my mind was oddly still. I felt weirdly relaxed. Relaxed but not relaxed – kind of pole-axed – nerves under control, but not under *my* control. The Kalmasol was stopping my mind racing, forcing it to slow right down, keeping my thoughts in check like turnstiles filtering crowds at a stadium. I'd never felt so weirdly flat and docile in all my life. The drugs had turned my busy brain into an empty biscuit tin. Fears and worries were hammering at the door, but nobody was answering.

Filled another cup of water, lifted it so shakily to my lips, I spilled it over myself. Started running around the cell to keep warm, tripping like a drunk.

I wondered what time it was. Light in the window suggested mid-afternoon. Or mid-morning – God only knew.

Another hundred years passed and I heard footsteps and keys. Harry Headcase came in with a lunch tray. Looked around for my breakfast tray. Saw I hadn't touched it, but didn't comment. Motioned me to fetch the tray. I picked it up, handed it over.

'What time is it?' I whispered.

He didn't even look at me. Backing out the door, he put the tray down on a chair in the passage, locked me in and left.

I picked up the tray and put it down in the corner. The smell of gravy pricked my nose – the aroma of pastry and custard.

C'mon, whispered the tray, *give yourself a break*.

Sorry, pal, I replied, *you'll have to do better than that*.

My head felt like a punctured football – my belly a revolving cement-mixer. I sipped water and lay on the floor.

Harry Headcase returned, saw the untouched tray. Took it off me and left.

The room was all at once stifling. Or maybe I had a fever. Or was it the dope, or a cocktail of everything? I was hot and shivering at the same time, and then I noticed it was gloomy out the window – a black sky like the end of the world.

I must have dozed, because all of a sudden I was startled awake by the Predator's voice in the passage, and realized I'd been putting this moment off.

Harry Headcase was standing in the passage with a supper tray. The Predator signalled him to wait; he stepped into my cell and snapped his fingers – a signal for Harry to switch on the strip light above my head. Mr Strang clasped his hands behind his back and looked at me. You're supposed to stand when a whip enters a room. I calmly returned his gaze.

'Stand.'

I stood slowly.

'Where is it?'

I swallowed – throat dry.

'The letter, boy! The apology to Miss Rice-Bird.'

The Predator's eye zeroed in on the clipboard. 'Fetch.'

I moved too slowly – he brushed past me and scooped up the clipboard. Flicked one blank page after another.

'If that's how you want to play it, fine by me. But remember, you remain here, and will continue to remain here, until the letter's done.'

Pausing in the doorway, he smiled and said, 'You're not the first boy to take me on. You'll soon change your tune.'

Harry Headcase gave Mr Strang a respectful nod, swapped the supper tray for my untouched lunch tray and left, locking me in. I placed the supper tray in the corner, trying not to notice the clingfilmed sandwiches, mug of hot chocolate, digestive biscuit.

Light was being sucked out of the cell when Moses arrived to shadow me to the jacks. Under his gaze I washed, brushed my teeth and returned to find my bed roll, bedding and pyjamas waiting. He stood studying me while I made up my bed. Locks turned, bolts slammed. I undressed, put on my pyjamas and got into bed.

Silence – just the wind in the trees and rain coming in fits.

Lightning flashed in the high window, blitzing the cell. Each time it flashed, the light picked out a spider on the wall by my face. I imagined making friends with it, feeding it scraps to win its trust. I remembered a joke my grandad liked to tell, and wished I hadn't, because I hated it. I tried lying there not remembering it, but you try not remembering something. There was this lifer doing thirty years, and twenty-five years into his sentence he notices a spider living in his cell – takes another year to win its trust, and they become friends, and it sleeps every night in his beard and does little jigs to keep his spirits up, a kind of spider flamenco, and when his sentence is finally up, he packs his friend in a matchbox padded with tissue, pops it in his pocket and steps into the world a free man. Says to himself, 'I think I'll celebrate,' goes into a pub and orders a pint. While the barman has his back turned, he takes out the matchbox and coaxes the spider onto the counter, itching to show off its dance routine. When the barman returns, he says, 'Look what I got here!' And the barman sees the spider and brings his fists down – *smack!* Squashes the spider flat. 'Sorry about that, sir – hot weather brings 'em out.' God, I hate that joke.

As the lightning hit the wall, I leaned closer and realized it wasn't a spider – it was *lettering*. In the next flash I made out the letters TT. What could it mean? Somebody's initials? Somebody banged up in here? Then it hit me – Tony Trevino! After his brave but dismal escape attempt, he was in here for four days and nights – just under a hundred hours, a Dovedale record – before breaking down and begging to be let out. He must have lain here and scratched his initials for courage. I lay back, trying to work out how many hours *I'd* done. Twenty-seven? Twenty-eight? Then I fetched the pen old Strang had given me, got down and scrawled MK beside the TT, and for some reason felt a rush of energy!

Knelt facing the window, closed my eyes and prayed to the Dude upstairs:

'Boss, do us a favour, give us this day the strength to hold out, and deliver us from visions of cold milk on cornflakes, and whipped cream and pancakes – rice and peas and chip butties – saussies and mustard, sponge pud and custard, mango sorbet dripping down my chin on a sunny afternoon . . .'

A rumble of thunder shook the night – a flash of lightning blinded me.

Was that a yes, boss?

Rain drummed in the darkness. I listened to the storm, remembering how once, when Dad was away during a bad one, Mum took me into her bed and held me tight, not because *I* was scared, but because *she* was. Another flash of lightning – a long drawn-out rattle of thunder.

Don't worry, Mum. I gotcha.

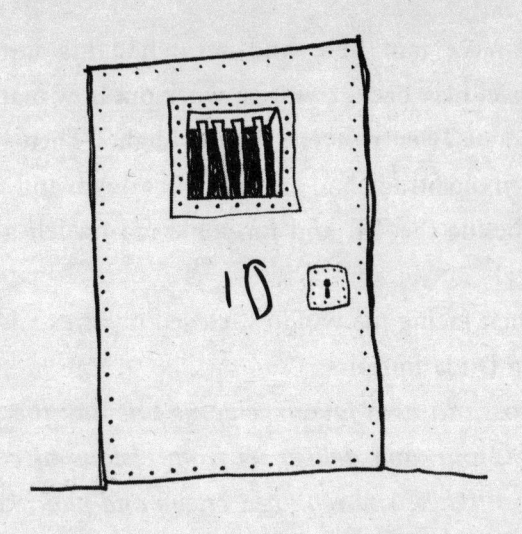

Two more days crept by and still I didn't eat. Dr Doughnut arrived to deal me my dope, and apart from sipping water and seeing double, that was it. I was starting to get whacked by monster headaches, and when I stood up the room went with me. Why was I refusing food? I wasn't too sure. I didn't plan it, or think of it as a hunger strike, it was just an impulse – an instinctive way of resisting.

Old Moses was standing there. I didn't even hear him come in. Shaking his head at another untouched tray.

'Relax, Mr Trust – Jesus managed it for forty days.'

'Son of God,' whispered Moses. 'You're just a poor sinner.'

He handed me a Bible – squinted at me. 'You pray?'

'Sometimes.'

'Pray to God—' he said, locking me in, 'but continue to row to the shore.'

My turn to shake my head. The things that geezer came out with!

I tried to collect my thoughts, drag some sense out of my drug-slugged head. As the hours drifted by, old Moses's words echoed in my head. *Pray to God, but continue to row to the shore* – like it's all right to ask for help, but don't expect him to do all the work. You're in charge – you got the power. It sort of helped me through the day, and the next day, the idea of praying for help but helping yourself at the same time.

In a strange way, I felt Clarence Trust rooting for me.

On day four I woke with my head clear as a bell. Also noticed the hunger pangs had settled. I felt very light and strange, looking down at myself from a height – an interesting feeling, like being dead and alive at the same time – a spirit floating in the material world. Maybe this was what it was like being dead. I felt I could wander through walls and zoom over treetops.

I didn't try it – I wasn't that confident.

They kept bringing my meals – I kept ignoring them. The devilish trays never let up: *Oi, Marcus, juicy burger and chips with lashings of ketchup, followed by two delicious scoops of ice cream – what do you say to that?*

'Shuddup!' I said. 'Just shuddup!'

I admit I was impressed. In all the time I'd been in

Dovedale, I never once saw two scoops of anything. Boys arrived at Dovedale carrying rolls of spare flesh and left lean as whippets. Despite regular food parcels, Ravi had lost a stone and had the makings of a cool dude. So listen up, mums and dads – if you're worried about your son's weight, pack him off to Dovedale, that's my advice. Now's good, while the offer lasts. With our carefully formulated programme of Discipline, Drugs and Direction, you never know, he might even return with his head screwed back on. I mean, look at mine!

Round and round the cell I roamed, concentrating on my breathing, monitoring my thoughts – the ones that said, *They're going to grind you down*, and the ones that said, *Rubbish – you can win this.*

Footfalls – belonging to more than one person. Harry Headcase opened up and stood back. In stepped the Predator, eyes hard with anger.

I stood facing him facing me.

He put his hands behind his back. I did the same.

'Chin up – shoulders straight!'

I obeyed. He leaned closer, freezing me with his eyes.

'You think you're so superior, but let me tell you something, you're a child of exceptional immaturity, and this little performance impresses no one, least of all me, and I've a good mind to force-feed you myself. Where is it?' he snapped, then strode over and picked up the clipboard. 'It had better be done this time.'

He stared at the top sheet, on which I'd sketched Bob Marley with a head of fabulous dreadlocks, holding a guitar which resembled a machine gun unleashing a hail of musical notes at a man bearing a surprising resemblance to . . . Mr Strang.

Fear gripped me. 'I meant to do the letter, sir, but . . .'

'But what?'

'I dunno, I just couldn't find the time.'

Silence. I felt the Predator at my back – braced myself for a whack round the head. Instead he breathed in my ear, 'If I had my way, I'd thrash you to within an inch of your life. Unfortunately, it's no longer permitted. Big mistake.' At the door, he turned. 'I'm not finished with you, Mr King . . . not by a long chalk.'

Harry Headcase slid my bolts and locked me in for another night.

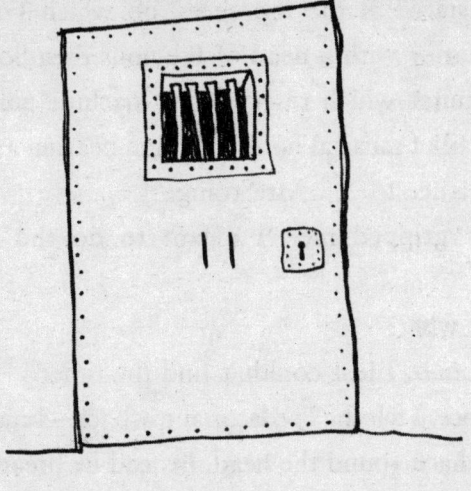

Day five. Another breakfast untouched. The trays didn't bother me any more. We weren't even on speaking terms.

Time washed over me. The fasting was outdoing the Kalmasol. Aside from stomach pains and bouts of dizziness my body felt clean, my heart calm, head clear. I felt relaxed, almost peaceful.

I sat against a wall, hugging my knees. Everything was simple now. Just sit it out.

A bird sang, over and over the same complicated refrain.

A sunbeam poked through the window and swept the floor.

I'm postponing your release indefinitely.

I wasn't bothered. Nothing bothered me, not even the closed and locked door. Everything was cool. By refusing their food I was taking back control.

I noticed the clipboard and paper on the floor. I bent down, unclipped a sheet, screwed it up and used it as a football.

Moses collected my untouched supper tray, and held the door open for a visitor. In stepped Dr Doughnut – white coat and bulky doctor's bag – humming to himself.

'Morning, Doc— Oops, sorry, not supposed to speak.'

'Morning, Malcolm – how are you?'

'Me, I'm fine – but I can't speak for Malcolm.'

'You'll make yourself ill, refusing to eat.'

'Maybe you should get somebody to amend your records?'

After making me take my two blue pills, Doc Doughnut instructed Moses to fetch two plastic chairs, and motioned me to sit while he took my pulse and blood pressure.

'Everything seems to be in order – but carry on like this and you'll do yourself serious damage, my boy,' he said, crossing his legs, uncrossing them and crossing them the other way. Then he took off his specs and breathed on one lens and then the other, polished vigorously and held up each in turn to the light. Not satisfied, he polished both lenses again – and finally put the specs back on, balanced them just so and took out my chart.

'I want you to promise to start eating.'

'Can we talk about the Kalmasol first, Doc? I don't need them.'

'Because otherwise I'm thinking we might have to re-jig your current dosage – reduce the K-M from two to one and put you on K-X . . . from tomorrow morning,' he said, making a note and rising to go.

'The K-M already fries my brains – what will I be like on the stronger stuff as well? No extra dope, Doc, please!' I pleaded, my way blocked by Moses.

Dr Doughnut walked off, whistling a cheery tune. Moses dropped a heavy hand on my shoulder – ushered me back into the cell.

'Calm down, son. Nowhere can a man find a quieter retreat than in his own soul.'

He locked me in for another night. I lay down. The thought of Kalmasol-M and X infecting my blood and storming my brain made me break out in a cold sweat. *My* veins, *my* brain. Just because a lad goes off the rails, what gives them the right to take possession of his body and tamper with his braincells?

There's a simple solution, I told myself. Stop this hunger strike.

No, I answered. This is my only means of resistance; this is all I got.

I curled myself up tight and shut my eyes and must have slept. Dreamed I was back in my old school, doing a test. Everyone else is writing furiously, but I'm stuck – the questions make no sense – they look like Japanese! 'Hey! Psst!' I go, trying to attract Shelly's help, but the teacher whips off his shades and points to the door, telling me to leave. Suits me – anything to get out of this. But then I notice the room has no door – or windows for that matter! How do I get *out*? How did I get *in*? I'm having trouble breathing; everybody else is breathing normally. Then, just as my head is about to explode, I jump up on my desk and, with an effort of sheer will, take off like a diver off a board, *upwards* – clean through the ceiling like a fist through a hat. Sky! Wide open sky . . .

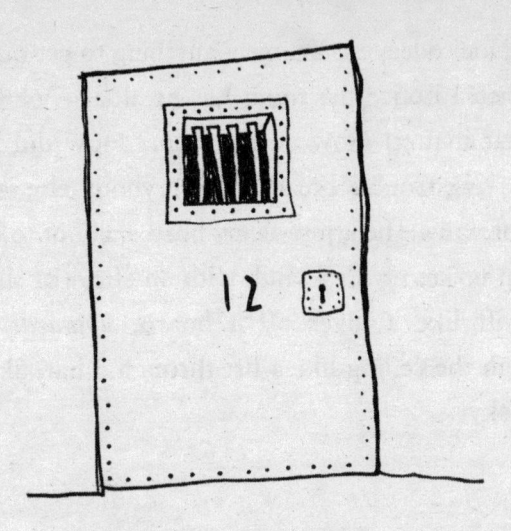

I sat up, heart thumping. Morning light hung in the high window. Old Moses escorted me to the jacks. Then he brought my breakfast, and the ironic look on his face told me the word was out that the doctor had persuaded me to eat. I thanked him and placed the tray in the corner for stray trays. My heart was beating fast. The tray was going, *Eat! EAT! Save yourself!*

I looked it in the eye, gangster-style. 'You talkin' to me? You talkin' to *me*?'

Old Moses frowned and left.

Before long, Dr Doughnut reappeared. At his shoulder, Harry Headcase carrying a jug of water, and I thought, *This doesn't look good.*

'Morning, young man,' said the doc. 'And how are we today?'

'Morning, Doc. Feeling good.'

'That's what we like to hear.'

'But I really don't need the extra dope, if that's OK with you.'

He smiled and held out a paper cup containing one blue tablet and one pink, the blue my usual K-M, the pink the heavy-duty K-X. Harry took the other cup from the doc, filled it with water and handed it back.

'Like I said, Doctor, I'm already Kalmasoled out of my brain, so if you don't mind—'

'Come now, Malcolm, we're not going to be difficult, are we?'

I became aware of Harry putting down the jug, removing his jacket and flexing his muscled arms. I met his gaze, which said, *Don't make me do this, son.*

'You're in a highly emotional state,' said the doc. 'Why not let these little fellows take the strain?'

I lowered my eyes, reached blindly for the cups. Put one, two pills in my mouth and washed them down.

'Show, dear boy . . . excellent fellow – thank you for your co-operation.'

The key turned, the bolts slammed, footsteps died.

I put a finger down my throat, but only succeeded in puking up froth. I started drinking water like mad – the whole jug, trying to wash the drugs from my system. I felt all right for a time and thought, We might be lucky. Then all at once I was queasy and shaking. The walls of the cell expanded and contracted – retreated and returned, closed in on me, slowly crushing my head. By the time lunch arrived, I was shaking so badly I was like a fool on a rolling deck and could barely carry the tray to the usual corner.

Every once in a while, the spy hole opened – and closed. I lay curled in a ball, shaking. Until the doctor's visit I'd been feeling good, I'd felt I was winning. But now they'd taken back control, I was back in their hands and in the grip of powerful drugs and I was depressed and getting more so by the minute. They were remorselessly turning the screw and I was getting crushed. They were bent on turning me into a docile sheep, and they were succeeding. Crazy thoughts threatened to overwhelm me, and as I lay twisting and moaning, I saw flames and black umbrellas, Mum, Dad and Clem at a graveside . . .

I vaguely heard someone at the spy hole, bolts drawn back, the door opening. What now? Someone was standing over me. I heard a rumble in his throat, and sat up.

Clarence Trust tilted his head and regarded me curiously, like you might a crazy but harmless creature. He was holding out a blanket.

'Sit up, son,' he said, stooping to drape the blanket round my shivering shoulders. 'What are you playing at? Is it so hard to say sorry?'

'If the Iceberg sent you because she's worried about Dovedale's reputation if something happens to me, you can forget it.'

'Nobody pulls my strings, son.'

'She's your boss.'

'I work for a bigger boss,' he said, flicking his eyes skywards.

He unslung a bag, took out a small basket and set it down on the floor. Then he turned the bag upside down and into the basket tumbled a load of tomatoes, all sizes, red, yellow and orange, and I remembered hearing how Moses lived in a mobile home somewhere up the lane past Mr Strang's cottage, and how he'd dug a vegetable patch out of the wilds and was growing all sorts.

'Pretty, don't you think?' he said, carefully arranging the display. 'If you don't feel like eating any, they might just cheer the place up.'

It *was* a pretty sight and I thanked him under my breath.

'If you *do* feel like having any, eat slowly, so you don't make yourself sick.'

I looked at him. 'How's Ravi doing?'

'Physically, fine.'

'Emotionally?'

'They wanted to put him in solitary, but the doctor feared for his health. His sentence has been extended by three months and like you he's had his visits suspended, so he's a bit down, as you can imagine.'

'Sentence extended' – I could only laugh – 'for getting mugged.'

Moses peered at me doubtfully. 'I saw those two boys' injuries, son.'

'Ah c'mon, Mr Trust, unpeel your senses. Why would clowns like us pick a fight with hoods like Bland and Litner? And would I be daft enough to smoke dope on my review day? They lied blind, they shafted us.'

He folded his massive arms and squinted at me. 'What happened?'

'They jumped Ravi in the woods and started beating him, and like a fool I ran back to help, and somehow, between us, we creamed them.'

Moses went, 'Hmm,' and rubbed his chin.

'I can't understand how your God can make people like that,' I said.

'Wasn't God starved them of love.'

'Who says they were starved?'

Moses smiled – I shivered under my blanket.

'He doesn't create bullying children – we do.'

'Then what was all that bull about original sin, Mr Trust?'

Old Moses looked up at the strip of sky and smiled. 'Yes, I'm becoming aware of a contradiction there somewhere. But why didn't you tell the Director the truth?'

'Listening's not her best event.'

'If what you say is true—'

'You don't believe me?'

'Actually, I do – you could have looked the other way. Instead you risked everything to help a friend.

Litner and Bland would never have done that.'

'I could cheerfully kill them.'

Old Moses chuckled deep in his chest. 'I was about to commend you for being a good Samaritan.'

'With my bare hands.'

'It's our *love* they need, son, not more violence. They've had plenty of that, believe me.'

'I got no time for people like that.'

'You like dogs?'

'Yes.'

'If a dog cringes when you go to stroke it, what does it tell you?'

'It's been mistreated.'

'Bland and Litner are like mistreated dogs.'

'A child's for life – not just for Christmas, right, boss?'

I started to cry – I couldn't help it. 'If we were mistreated dogs, Mr Trust, would you whips be giving us drugs to make us behave?'

He didn't answer.

'It's a joke, isn't it?' I said. 'School and education, Dovedale and rehabilitation – it's all a shining lie, and you're part of it, boss. You help keep it all going.'

He returned my gaze.

'Does your God approve of Dovedale? If he does, he's got serious issues.'

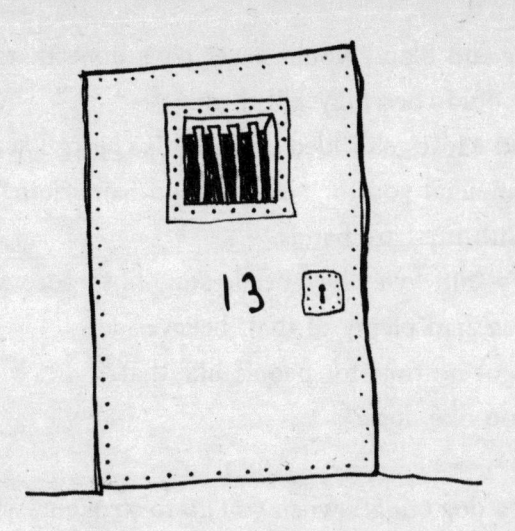

After he'd gone, I stood gazing up at the sky in the window. I felt lighter in my mind. Talking to Moses had unburdened me, even if talking to me had troubled him.

I looked at the basket on the floor, then picked up a bright red tomato and put it to my nose and sniffed it. It smelled fresh and spicy. I took a bite – 'Wow!'

When Moses arrived with my supper tray, he saw I'd eaten half the tomatoes. He smiled and left me in peace. I sat down with the supper tray – soup, bread rolls and a slice of cheese – and started to eat.

I should have listened to what he'd said about eating slowly – should have remembered those films where the famished hero stumbles on food, wolfs it down and is violently sick. I didn't vomit, but my belly swelled like a balloon and I lay groaning on the floor, and was still groaning when I sat down and started the letter. Tore it up and started again, until it read:

Dear Miss Rice-Bird,
I'm really sorry about what happened.
I'm nearly sure it won't happen again.
    Yours sincerely,
    Marcus King

It was as low as I was willing to go.

It was getting dark, my bed roll hadn't arrived and I was lying on the floor in a trance, longing to be back in the coop, going to breakfast and lessons as usual, when heavy footfalls and a voice I recognized made my blood run cold. I stood up.

Keys rang, locks rattled – enter the Predator.

'So! The boy has finally called off his childish protest. Where's the letter?'

I handed him the clipboard. It was a real page-turner – he read it at one sitting.

'This is no apology' – slapping the letter – 'this is a sly, impertinent attempt to wriggle out of an apology, and it deceives no one. Sit.'

I sat cross-legged on the floor.

Unclipping the letter, he tore it in two, in four and

finally into eight pieces, held them high and released a little blizzard over my head.

Weathering his gaze, I wondered what he got up to in his free time – hare-coursing? badger-baiting? – and what mysteries lay behind the locked door in his office where not even the cleaners were permitted to peek? Rumours varied from retired punishment canes to the bones of a boy killed in a rage.

Handing me the clipboard and pen, he said, 'Start writing,' and dictated the day's date, making me underline it with the ruler.

'*Dear Miss Rice-Bird,*' he continued, '*I sincerely regret . . . my appalling and violent conduct* – full stop. *I am extremely* – underlined – *sorry to have let you down . . . and I promise there will be no repetition . . . of my disgraceful behaviour* – full stop. *Yours faithfully . . .* and sign it.'

He grabbed the clipboard and checked it.

'Could have saved ourselves a lot of trouble, couldn't we? Collect your things and return to your dormitory.'

'Sir?'

'What?'

'Do I still have to spend another six months in Dovedale?'

'Definitely.'

'What if the ambush never happened? What if it wasn't my spliff?'

'I'm not interested.'

'What if those scumbags suffer from Compulsive Lying Disorder—?'

'Move!'

I made my way slowly up to the coop, shocked how easily the Predator had forced my hand – cheered by the thought that I'd gone the distance, made him sweat for his victory. He'd beaten me, no question, yet he seemed somehow less intimidating than before – not less dangerous, maybe *more* dangerous, but no longer quite as invincible. Victory had weakened him. Defeat had made me stronger. Except physically. I was *wrecked*. Five or six days – I'd lost count – without food, combined with the effects of high-dose Kalmasol had done me in.

My coopmates were getting into their pyjamas.

'Don't look so spooked. It's only me, trimmer and slimmer from my stint in the slammer. How you feeling, Rav?'

There was a weird atmosphere in the room I couldn't put a finger on.

'I said, how you doing?'

'What a bloody travesty, believing them and locking you up. This place is a disgrace – there! The start of a rap for you!'

'Keep away from him, Marco,' said Archie. 'They forget his dope.'

'So busy plying me with exotic medications,' Ravi

confirmed, 'they forgot my Kalmasol! I'm going to speak to my lawyer!'

'You didn't remind them?'

'Are you *mad*! I'm *me* again – it's absolutely wonderful!'

With that he seized me round the waist and waltzed me round the room, singing loudly in Italian, '*La-la-la-stupendo! La-la-la meraviglioso!*'

'Whoa! Take it easy, bro!'

'Rat-catcher,' said Shelly. 'Rat-catcher!'

Old Moses appeared in the doorway – a doom-laden stare.

'My fault entirely, Mr Trust!' puffed Ravi. 'I must have been a songbird in a previous life.'

'You'll be plankton in the next, you all will, if you continue to shun the light. Forget something, Mr King?' Waving my Bible.

'You're a star, Mr Trust. And thanks for all the advice.'

'Many receive good advice, son – few profit by it.'

He dealt us another warning look and left. My coop-mates sort of sniggered.

'I heard they topped up your sentence, Rav?'

They all looked at me. There was a bad smell of avoidance in the air.

'Yes' – panic in Ravi's eyes – '*three months, three bloody months* – and for what? For getting assaulted by a pair of mad thugs – it's too much, it's really too much!'

'Don't worry, Ravi, we'll get you through, won't we, lads?'

'I'll die in here – so help me.'

A sudden silence.

'Did they really stick *six* extra months on you, Marcus?' murmured Shelly.

'Minimum. I'll be here when you dudes are long gone.'

They didn't know where to look.

'You wanna start taking care of number one, Marco,' said Archie.

'I'll try and remember that.'

'Bet you crawled,' he said.

'Forget him, he's jealous,' said Shelly. 'A hundred and twenty hours you did down there. Tony Trevino did ninety-eight. You broke the record, man – by a mile.'

'Bet Strang made you squirm,' sneered Archie.

To which I replied:

> *'I may have signed the letter,*
> *But he had to wave a hammer.*
> *He even wrote it for me,*
> *'Cos he didn't like my grammar.'*

'*And you never shed a tear,*' Ravi concluded passionately, '*even though you missed your mama!*'

'Marcus the slammer champ!' cried Shelly, coming to shake my hand.

'The slummer chump!' cried Ravi, clasping me in a fierce embrace. 'You had us worried, old chap.'

'You had *me* worried, Rav, when you collapsed in the woods.'

'Don't! I thought I was going to die,' roared Ravi, wrapping himself magnificently in a bed sheet. 'Kneel!' he commanded.

'What?'

Rolling his eyes – 'You don't say *what*! You say, *Forgive me, your liege, I didn't quite catch that*. Kneel, imbecile!'

I knelt.

'You, my faithful servant,' he cried, 'came to my aid when brigands assaulted me. As if this wasn't gallant enough, you endured the Beast of Dovedale's foul dungeon for longer than anyone in antiquity, and have returned to us a *legend*, and from now on' – touching me on either shoulder with a plastic coat hanger – 'you shall be known as *Sir* Noodle Head.'

Shelly and Archie cheered and applauded, and Ravi continued, 'Arise, Sir Noodle! And to demonstrate the depth of your gratitude, I invite you to kiss my—'

Bum, he was going to say, twisting round and dropping his pyjama bottoms, when Archie cried, 'Rat-catcher!'

Rapid steps, Moses!

'What the devil's going on? We can hear you upstairs.'

'A thousand penances, sir,' said Ravi. 'We were just welcoming the champion home.'

'The new record holder,' said Shelly.

'Hmm,' grunted Moses, pointing at the clock. 'Five minutes to get your miserable backsides to bed.'

'Good Lord,' crooned Ravi, 'I had better convey my royal behind to the lavatorium without delay.'

Gathering up washbags, we scuttled to the bathroom. I sidled in next to Ravi at the sinks.

'Why didn't you speak up for us, Rav?'

'What?'

'Why didn't you tell Harry Headcase what went on in the wood?'

Ravi speechless.

'Why, Ravi, why?'

'Are you crazy?' Hissing at me in the mirror. 'Are you completely off your noodle? Bland and Litner made it abundantly clear what would happen to me if I breathed a word. Believe me, Marcus' – eyes welling up – 'I wanted nothing more than to see us spared and those ulcerous swine punished, but I was frankly petrified and still am. Look at me!' He groaned at his reflection. 'This is what I have to live with, this fat trembling fool, frightened day and night . . .'

He was shaking – I was shaking. I laid a hand on his shoulder.

'It's OK, Rav . . . *you're* scared, *I'm* scared, we're all scared. Hey, listen, you slobs' – swinging round and pointing at my coopmates, and lowering my voice as a crowd of other slogs arrived with washbags – 'that's why we gotta stick together, you with me? United we thrive – divided we dive!'

Back in the coop, during Quiet Time, I got out of bed and looked through the barred window at the gardens and gravel and the trees beyond and murmured, 'I'm getting out of here.'

'What's that?' whispered Shelly.

'I've been thinking about it . . . I've had plenty of time to think.'

Everything had gone strangely quiet, and I thought it was because of what I'd said, but when I looked, there were two avenging angels in the doorway. Checking the coast was clear, Skinny Hitler entered the coop, Strangeboy on his shoulder. Not a pretty sight, Strangeboy with his slitty eyes and flab, Skinny Hitler pale as a corpse, eyes like flick-knives. They each carried a spiked hairbrush and had eyes only for me.

'I'm disappointed in you,' said Skinny, 'spreading lies about what happened in the wood.'

'Payback time,' said Strangeboy, slapping the brush in the palm of his hand.

'A couple of days in the slammer,' jeered Skinny. 'Call that punishment?'

'And what did Strang's boots taste like, eh?' Strangeboy chuckled.

A moment's suspense, to jack up the fear. Then, just

as they were about to move in, and just as I was casting about for a weapon, a voice piped up from under his covers. 'Marco don't lick boots.'

It was Archie – and the unexpected intervention surprised everyone.

'And he broke the record.'

The two goons looked at Archie and belly-laughed.

'Yes, and your despicable lies put Marcus in there,' said Shelly, sitting up.

The laughter stopped. The goons stared at him.

'And in case the word *despicable* is beyond you,' said Ravi, swinging his bulk out of bed and planting his feet on the floor, 'it means cowardly and spineless – so permit me to inform you that next time you do the dirty on us – you unseemly slimeballs, you fulminating fascists! – we won't just thrash you, we'll slice you up so your mothers won't recognize you – that's if you have mothers, which I strongly doubt.'

The raiders stood dumbstruck.

'Yo, Ravi! Some friggin' speech!' I cried, jumping across to hit him with high fives. Then I glanced at Archie and Shelly, and they twigged and got out of bed – and the four of us stood shoulder to shoulder in a seething wall until the thugs – exchanging glances – shrewdly withdrew.

United we stand!

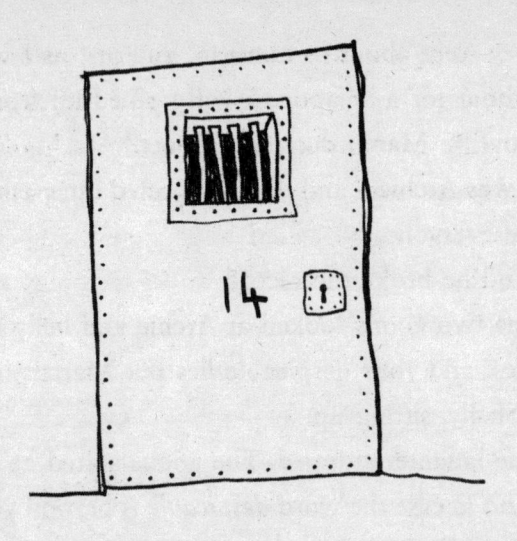

Watching the door in case the swine returned, I lay listening to the night – wind in the trees, water gurgling in pipes.

My thoughts were dark. I'd done all I could to stay out of trouble, but what was the use? I was a marked man. I could knuckle down for another six months and the same could happen again – one incident or another turned against me. I began to suspect that Miss Rice-Bird, Mr Strang and even Dr Cavendish guessed what had really gone on in Strapps Wood and didn't care, because their agenda was to break boys who ask too many questions. Genuine delinquents like Bland and Litner were easy meat, but I was a free spirit, that was my crime, and they wouldn't be satisfied until I broke down and marched in step with everyone else. The authorities don't fear thugs; they have all the resources they need to contain them. They fear young people impertinent enough to think for themselves, students demanding a say in the running of their schools, young people eager to be active participants, not passive consumers. The very idea of giving them responsibility freaks the control freaks. Let's keep things safe: Do this, do that, and whatever you do, don't think for yourself. And if you kick up a fuss, we'll label you attention-seeking and hyperactive. And if you try and escape, we'll run you down and dope you up and call it rehabilitation.

It was time to jump ship. The thought thrilled and terrified me.

It was only a matter of logistics and timing – and whether or not to let my coopmates in on it. I really liked the idea of the four of us checking out of the hotel together, but even if they were willing, it was hard to imagine Ravi keeping up, or Archie not totally blowing it. Shelly was a different matter. If he was on for it, he'd keep running and never stop. *I'd* be the one struggling to keep up.

But right now I was in bad shape – in no condition to plan a breakout, never mind carry it out. My head was Kalmasoled, my body drained. I needed to get off the dope and get fit. How not to take the daily dope – that was the challenge.

Next thing I knew it was 6.30 and I was being blasted awake by the alarm. But today felt different – we all *bounced* out of bed – there was a new energy in the alley: we felt great, we felt huge, we felt intense pride at having faced down those gangsters last night.

'Look how far we've come!' I cried, as we stumbled laughing to the bathroom. 'We tragic slogs who used to hate each other – together we scared off the Dovedale Mafia.' We didn't care how cold it was for a summer's morning, we felt super-cool, *invincible*. We could handle anything they threw at us.

But soon as I joined the queue for a sink, Moses stopped me.

'Mr King?'

'Morning, boss.'

'Rule infringement.'

'I was in when the bell stopped.'

'Your feet, son, your feet.'

I looked down. 'What's wrong with them?'

Slippers. I'd forgotten my regulation slippers, a punishable offence. I fully expected a hundred lines, but instead he jerked his cannonball head – 'Go get 'em.'

I thanked him and ran. Doubled back in my old codger's slippers, and was surprised when Moses stopped me again.

'You're late.'

'What?'

'Back to base.'

'You're having me on.'

'One hundred and fifty press-ups.'

'You got no right.'

'No, my friend, you're the only one with no rights in this equation.'

I gazed at him. 'What's going on, chief?'

'Orders.'

He didn't need to spell it out. I saw it clearly, the Predator calling a meeting of whips on how to deal with me.

The slippers palaver made me late. I slid into the dining hall with seconds to spare and joined the end of the dope line. As my turn arrived, I noticed Harry Headcase and the Predator standing by, arms folded, watching. Dr Doughnut smiled and shook two tablets into a cup – pink and blue – and waited for me to open my mouth.

'I took your advice, Doc, and started eating – so why the pink?'

'Open up, there's a good chap.'

'With respect, you gave me the impression that if I dropped my protest—'

'Oh, for goodness' sake!' Doughnut snapped, and Harry Headcase and the Predator moved in, grabbed my arms and bent me backwards over a table. I lashed out, and the struggle to contain me brought the hall to its feet. The Predator didn't mind cereal bowls shattering on the floor – he relished the public humiliation of a rebel. With everyone in the hall on their feet, jeering and booing, Harry Headcase held me down, the Predator prised my jaws apart and Dr Doughnut dropped two pills in my mouth and poured water after, making me choke and splutter, spraying everyone.

The Predator jumped back, wiping his jacket. Silenced the mob with a look.

I stood up, shaken.

'Show,' said the doc.

I couldn't – I was trying to hide the pills under my tongue.

'Right, fine!' said the Predator. 'Back to isolation.'

'No!'

'Did you say something, boy?'

'I really don't wanna go back there – please.'

'I'm still not hearing you.'

'Sir.'

'So we're going to co-operate from now on, are we, Mr King?'

'Absolutely . . . sir.'

'Good. Repeat after me: I shall co-operate fully from now on.'

'I shall co-operate fully from now on . . . sir.'

'Show, dear boy,' said the doc.

I swallowed and showed.

The eyes of slogs, whips and kitchen staff followed me back to my place in disgrace. But beneath the hot skin and watering eyes, I was cool. No trailing off with my tail between my legs, that's not my style. If I did the stupidest thing in the world, if I accidentally pulled the plug on the entire planet, I'd still hold my head up. Every eye in the hall watched as I reached for the milk and poured some over my porridge. My hands trembled, but my soul was cool.

The struggle's not over – it's just beginning.

I looked up for the sugar. Shelly, sitting across the table, pushed the bowl over to me. I met his eye and felt a glow of gratitude for his small gesture. All around me slogs drowned porridge in milk and sugar and ate like dogs. From a distant table came Skinny Hitler's mocking voice –

'So we're going to co-operate from now on, are we . . . sir?'

I ignored him. *I'm getting out of here – just you watch.*

The pink pills generally took about ten, fifteen minutes to work. Some boys said they didn't notice any-thing, but then they wouldn't have noticed if their brains had been surgically removed and replaced by pizza dough. With me it was worse some days than others. One day I'd get this harmless tingling all over, the next violent shakes and double vision. The cocktail of K-M and K-X also affected some worse than others. It made my brain stop-start, every thought interrupting itself like an out-of-tune piano – or taking a couple of seconds longer, like one of those dinosaurs whose noodle was located so far from its bum, it took it a couple of seconds to unscramble vital news, like, *Uh, I think somebody's just taken a bite out of my tail.*

I had to think of a way of not taking the stuff, but how are you supposed to think with a scrambled brain?

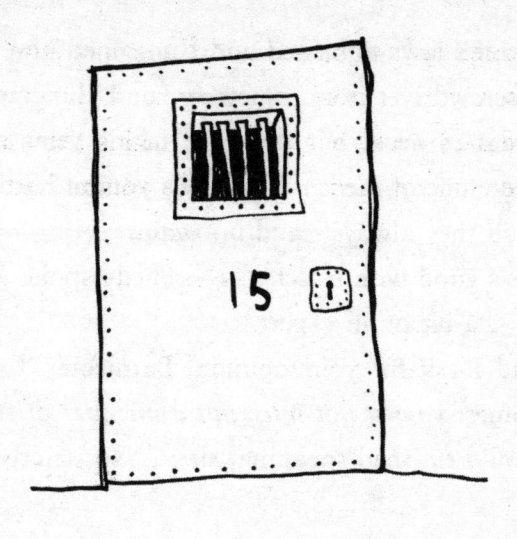

At eight twenty-five on the morning after my release from solitary, by the clock above the coop door, we set off for class. Or started to, until Mr Strang blocked our way.

'Stand by,' he ordered, and each boy doubled back and stood to attention at the foot of his bed. He began with Archie.

'Yes, well, what can one say?'

Archie's personal bed space was always a disaster. They'd tried every kind of penalty until they realized he wasn't lazy or defiant, he simply couldn't make a bed or fold a shirt to save his life. Even now, as Sir pointed at Archie's slippers and said, 'Can't you see they're the wrong way round?' Archie shrugged hopelessly.

'In all my born days' – Sir sighed – 'I have never encountered such a dunce.'

Archie's jaws tightened and I imagined him conjuring a screwdriver from somewhere and plunging it into Mr Strang's neck, but the dope in his veins steadied him, like one of those rubber dolls you hit hard as you like and they always stand up again.

'He's good with insects, sir' – Shelly spoke up recklessly – 'a bit of an expert.'

'Did I ask for your opinion, Barnicote? Two hundred lines: *I must not interrupt a member of staff.*'

'You'd finished speaking, sir . . . so strictly speaking—'

'Another two hundred.'

Shelly blushed and then paled, and I thought, That reminded him of his dad, but again the dope did its work. Shelly withdrew into himself, crushed and silent.

The Predator inspected Shelly's immaculate area without a word and moved smartly on to Ravi's kingdom, where an offending object on top of the chest of drawers caught his eye. He held it up between thumb and forefinger.

'An apple pip, Mr Sharma. Evidence of fruit consumed?'

'Good Lord, no, sir. More likely a bird brought it in.'

'Don't let me find one again.'

'Absolutely not, sir, thank you, sir. And may I be so bold as to enquire—'

'What?'

'Whether, in all other respects, you find my personal space satisfactory?'

'I find the personal space you take up excessive, Mr Sharma. Get to class.'

Ravi bowed his head. We started to leave.

'Did I say *you*?'

Clicking his fingers, Mr Strang motioned me to return to my post. As the others left, he started with my bed. Annoyed that he could find nothing wrong with it, he seized the pillow, pyjamas and covers and flung them violently to the floor. Then he tore back the bed sheet and threw it after, and started on my chest of drawers.

'Permission to speak, sir.'

'Denied.'

Observing my perfectly placed slippers, he toe-poked them out of line – 'Not straight.' Ran a finger across the top of my spotless chest of doors – 'Filthy.'

We'd all seen this routine before, and been driven – at one time or another – to the verge of tears. But I wasn't going to give him the satisfaction.

Opening my top drawer, he lifted out my framed photo, showing Mum and Dad cavorting like kids on Brighton beach. The Predator turned the picture frame over, unclipped the back and discovered a second photograph, some pretty black chick I'd cut from a magazine, and looked at secretly before lights out.

'What's this?'

'She was advertising Caribbean Airways, or something.'

'What's the rule about photographs?'

'One, but—'

'We appear to have two here. Your mathematics is slipping. I shall have to talk to Miss Cumberland. Meanwhile,' he said, tearing the pretty black model in two, and then in four, and letting the pieces drop, 'two hundred lines of *I must keep my personal bed space tidy* and another two hundred of *I must obey the one photograph rule*.' Then he liberated the rest of my drawers, pitching every item of clothing on the floor. Something caught his attention. Damn! I thought, and watched him undo a pair of socks and find my three Brighton beach pebbles hidden inside.

'Haven't I met these before?'

'They're not breaking any rule.'

'Potential weapons.' Pocketing them.

'Just lucky charms.'

'Five minutes to get your space in order,' he said, turning on his heels.

'They belong to me! You've no right!'

He stopped in the doorway and turned. 'You're sadly mistaken, Mr King. When you came here, you forfeited your rights. And that's another two hundred lines of *I must never raise my voice to a member of staff*. That's six hundred lines, and I'll have them by this time tomorrow.'

He held my gaze and left, and I got down and collected every bit of torn-up magazine photo and put them
in my pocket. Then I put my parents back in their frame,
and looked at the shambles all around and wanted to
scream, wanted to hurl my chest of drawers through
the window. Instead, I sat cross-legged on my bed and
shut my eyes and got a handle on my breathing. Minutes
passed and I sat there seething, not caring what the
Predator said or did when he returned. I cursed myself
for losing control and realized with a shock that I was
close to cracking, and that that was exactly what he
wanted.

Footsteps. Someone coming up the stairs. I braced
myself. Stay cool this time – stay cool.

'Merciful God – what's going on here?'

It was Clarence Trust, and he knew perfectly well.

'Shouldn't you be off watering your vegetables,
boss?'

'You're running late, son,' he said, getting down to
start picking up the mess. 'Let's put your house back
in order.'

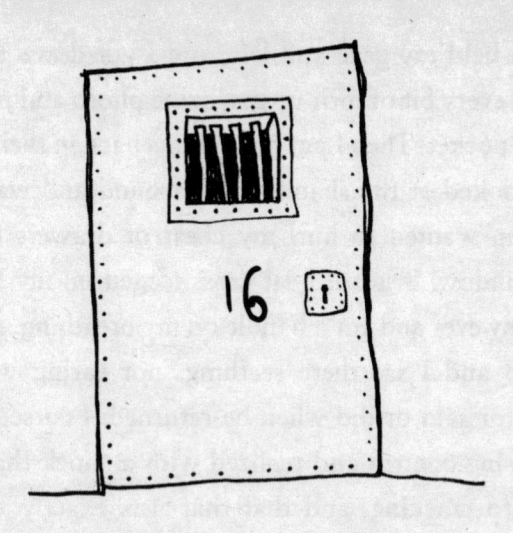

Miss Cumberland seemed pleased to see me – 'Welcome back, Marcus! We missed you.' But she was distracted, trying to stop a fight breaking out between my coopmates and the other four angels we shared the class with.

She tried again to get the lesson off the ground, but the moon was in the wrong place, or our Kalmasol mix wasn't working, or else it was just another morning in Dovedale. The strain was in her eyes. She returned to her desk and went very quiet, gazing out the window.

'She's having a sulk,' Archie jeered.

I looked out at the distant hills, thinking, A week or two from now, whatever happens, I'll be out of here, dead of night, heading south. I looked at Alice. What a waste of a lovely teacher. Unlike her predecessor, who told me to see the doctor if I had a problem, Alice kept the door open for me at all times. If someone came in and closed it on the way out, she'd give me the nod to open it again.

'I'm not stupid, you know,' she said. 'Nor as soft as some of you think. It's just that I believe in *self*-discipline.'

'You mean whipping ourselves, miss?' gasped Ravi. 'The board of governors might have something to say about that.'

'It means taking responsibility for your own behaviour, not waiting for me or Mr Strang to control you with threats.'

'Wasting your time, miss' – I smiled – 'it'll never work.'

'I think you're wrong, Marcus—' she started to say, and saw I was messing.

Good old Alice, she always tried to make lessons interesting, and when we misbehaved, instead of punishing us, found creative ways of dealing with it, like putting us on trial for minor infringements.

'Dropping sweet papers on the classroom floor is a serious offence,' she'd say gravely. 'How do you plead, Mr Sharma?'

'I beg your pardon?'

'That's not a plea – pick a defence team!'

So there's Ravi on trial for dropping sweet papers, with me as his barrister and Shelly the pompous prosecution, assisted by Archie, whose contribution was to keep pointing at Ravi, saying, 'Guilty! You can tell by looking at him.'

Alice started setting up more compelling scenarios – me on trial for drug-dealing; Shelly up before the military draft board, trying to avoid going to war by dressing as a girl; and even Archie stopped taking the mick and got involved when he found himself accused of burning down Dovedale Hall, with half the whips and slogs burned to a crisp.

Alice was on our side. This earned her enemies. Her idea of rehabilitation clashed with theirs. She thought love could move mountains. She thought love could rehabilitate young offenders.

A couple of days after my slammer release, as we were working in pairs doing spontaneous role-play – X a parent and Y a son caught with a packet of condoms – the door flew open.

'Morning, Mr Strang,' said Alice. 'As you can see, we're doing—'

'Drama, Miss Cumberland? Forgive me, but I thought we agreed that—?'

She tried to take him aside, we heard her murmur the word *therapeutic*, but he laid into her like she was an unruly pupil –

'Don't ever let me catch you doing drama again, Miss Cumberland – is that understood?'

After he'd gone, we sat in silence, robbed of the one subject that took us out of ourselves and let us soar above the petty and the bitter and the dope. It shocked us that Miss Wonderland was as powerless as us.

Or was she? She didn't seem to know when she was beaten. When one door slammed, she tried another.

'How would some of you like to go on an outing?'

We looked up – *What?*

She had a contact working with disabled teenagers near a seaside town over the border in Scotland. How would we like to spend a day working with them?

'How would we know where to begin?' said Ravi, nervous of anything new.

'Fiona and I would be with you all the time.'

'Sounds like hard work,' someone groaned.

'An adventure!' said Alice. 'An experience you'll never forget.'

Little did she guess how right she'd be.

'So what's the idea?' said Shelly.

'Broaden your outlook . . . experience humanity in all its remarkable forms.'

'How disabled is *disabled*?' wondered Ravi.

'Some mentally – some physically.'

'I'm not working with geeks and nutters, miss,' said Archie.

'If you're going to even think that way, I'm not taking you.'

'And I hate heights, miss – how many times have I told you?'

Alice looked at him blankly. 'I'm sorry, Archie, you've lost me.'

'Scotland?' he said. 'Mountains?'

'It's by the sea, Archie – sea level.'

'All right, but I'm not getting in a plane.'

'Archie, Scotland's just up the road.'

'If there was a TV show called *Sawdust Mind*,' sighed Ravi, 'where dimwits compete to see who knows the least—'

'Thank you, Ravi, that'll do,' said Alice.

'Sounds cool,' I said, 'but will they really let us out?'

'Miss Rice-Bird is giving it serious thought.'

'That means no.'

'She's a Christian and I suggested it would be good for you to meet some of God's less fortunate children.'

'Good move, miss. But she's not going to let me out.'

'You did your time in the slammer and you wrote a letter of apology.'

'Wasn't thinking of that.'

'Yes, we could have a problem there, Marcus. I'd need your word that you wouldn't run off.'

'You got it.'

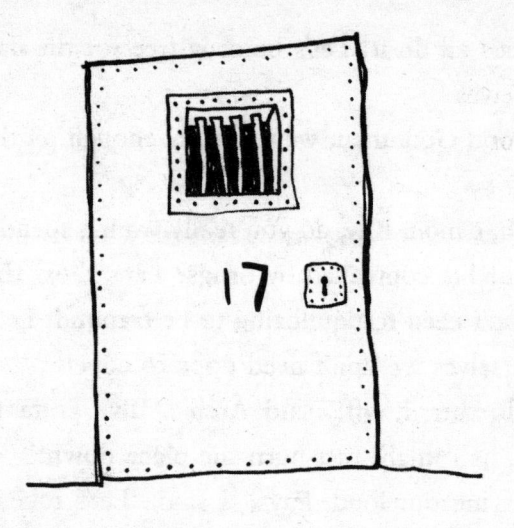

Miss Rice-Bird was nervous about the outing. If something happened, it would reflect badly on Dovedale. Alice argued it didn't say much for Dovedale if a hand-picked party of medicated and supervised Dovedale students couldn't be trusted to conduct themselves properly for a few hours. She was throwing down a challenge. She believed in us and was confident the day would be a great success. The Iceberg grudgingly gave her blessing, but for a maximum of four boys.

Alice suggested me and my coopmates. Shelly and I were keen; Ravi and Archie needed coaxing.

Right, that's it, I thought. Ideal time to test my no-Kalmasol trick. I spoke to the others after lights out.

'Let's all do it! Let's be drug-free for the day – our real selves.'

'Good God, man, we're barmy enough *on* the damn stuff!'

'Ah, c'mon, Rav, do you really wanna spend the rest of your life controlled by drugs? Let's show the world we don't need tranquillizing to be tranquil! Let's prove to ourselves we don't need dope to cope!'

'Ah, turn it off!' said Archie. 'I've gotta take me meds, or I might just burn the place down!'

'Crying out loud, guys,' I said. 'Let's take control! Just for a couple of days, that's all I'm asking.'

They were nervous and maybe a little excited.

'How's it done?' said Shelly.

'Wait!' I said, and got everyone kneeling in the middle of the coop, hands on hands and swearing secrecy.

'Spit it out,' Shelly pressed me.

'To outwit our friend Dr Doughnut,' I whispered, 'we'll need to get hold of something that's strictly illegal in Dovedale.'

'*What*?'

'Chewing gum. That's where your talent comes in, Archie.'

'Which one? I'm loaded.'

I reminded everyone that Dovedale caretaker Yardley Giles was always chewing gum, and smiled at Archie.

'Tricky,' said Archie. 'Very tricky.'

'Don't gimme grief,' I said, mock-gangster. 'You got forty-eight hours.'

'How long's that?'

Days passed. I remained focused on getting mind and body ready for my escape. Every minute of our twice-weekly periods in Dovedale's tragic library I spent digging out scraps of information on the local area – locations of farms, hill-walking trails – anything.

Flicking through a newspaper one day, Shelly stumbled on an amazing find; he glanced up at Mrs Armitage – the Iceberg's fearsome secretary who doubled as the librarian – and ambled over to show me, pointing at a particular article.

Mrs Armitage peered over her specs, Shelly drifted away and my eyes were drawn to a headline: UN CRITICIZES BRITAIN'S TREATMENT OF CHILDREN. A United Nations report

> expressed alarm at the steadily rising number of children and teenagers being held in detention centres, and concern at the extent to which juvenile institutions in the UK were generally poorly staffed, with bullying, self-harm and suicides prevalent . . .

It also lashed out at what it called 'the unacceptable rates of recidivism in detention centres for offenders aged 14 to 16'.

They could have been referring to Dovedale, but didn't mention names, except for some place called Risinghill in Suffolk, which they praised as 'an open institution with a progressive programme of outward bound courses, personal development, supportive staff and low rates of recidivism'. Risinghill regularly turned out young people who went on to hold down jobs, while too many detention centres were little better than 'universities of crime and despair'.

What exactly was recidivism? A disease triggered by poor nutrition? Mental breakdown? I approached the desk.

'Could I borrow a dictionary, please?'

Mrs Armitage removed her glasses and looked at me. 'What for?'

You'd think I'd requested a stick of dynamite.

'I like learning new words.'

'You might start with *contrition*,' she suggested helpfully, and lifted down a book the size of a breeze block.

I carried it back to my table and found – '*recidivism*: A tendency to relapse into a former pattern of behaviour; especially a tendency to return to criminal habits'.

I gazed out the window, recalling something the Iceberg said at our first meeting – *Too many boys leave here and pursue a life of drugs and crime*. In other words Dovedale inmates, on release, had a chronic habit of re-offending, which didn't exactly fit the sales pitch. Dovedale Hall was a *failure*.

Before the period could end, I carefully removed – inch

by inch – the double sheet of newspaper containing the UN article, folded it under the table and slipped it into my pocket. That evening, during homework in the den, I cut the article out and sealed it inside a bookmark fashioned out of paper and sellotape. At bed time I transferred the bookmark to the Bible in my top drawer.

Meanwhile, Archie watched the caretaker like a pro – which pocket he kept his gum in, and how often he disposed of a chewed piece and reached for a new one. We'd ruled out using discarded gum – too disgusting. Archie made his move, taking great care because Yardley Giles was known as one of Strang's spies.

'Can I have a word, sir?' – interrupting the caretaker sweeping the front steps.

'Ah' – Giles leaning on his broom – 'the resident pyromaniac!'

'What?'

'No, you can't borrow my lighter!' the caretaker chuckled.

'*What?*'

'Never mind, Archie. We can't all be brain surgeons. What can I do for you?'

'I found this.'

Slowly opening his right hand to reveal a cigarette, Archie drew his victim's gaze away – leaving his left hand to work its mischief in the caretaker's pocket.

'Interesting – where?' demanded Yardley Giles, confiscating the offending article.

'On the ground.'

'*Where?*'

'Outside the staff room. Did I do right, sir?'

The caretaker rolled his eyes. Archie went on his way, innocently whistling.

Next morning, before going to breakfast, each of us chewed a stick of gum and joined the dope queue. I went first.

'Morning, Doc. Beautiful day!'

He blinked at me – it was lashing rain! I popped my pills one at a time, making a big thing about trying to swallow them, and, using my tongue as a lever, pressed them into the soft chewing gum wedged behind my front teeth.

'Show.'

I could feel the chewing gum slipping, and with it the pills.

'Wider.'

I opened my eyes wider.

'Your *mouth*, dear boy.'

With a cluck of impatience he poked his thumb in my mouth and peered in.

'Next.'

I stepped away. Shelly and then Archie successfully underwent the ordeal. Ravi froze. We watched, mesmerized. He was so nervous, someone had to push him up to Doughnut's trolley. Even then we could see him fumbling madly – gratefully taking his medicine. Shelly and Archie laughed, but to me it was spoiling the whole drug-free experiment. Ravi rejoined us, weak in the knees but smiling. Discreetly spitting two pills into his palm, he pocketed them.

'You did it!' I whispered.

None of us noticed any difference at first. Coming off Kalmasol wasn't like jumping from a moving vehicle and losing your balance; it was more like Asian flu creeping up on you. Within hours we were getting dizzy spells, headaches, rushes of manic energy – cold turkey without the trimmings. By the following evening, we were really spaced.

The Iceberg lined us up in her office in our pyjamas. Still suffering from the shock of no Kalmasol, we could barely stand.

'Regarding your trip the day after tomorrow – it's a treat and privilege you boys have scarcely earned. I've only agreed to it because Miss Cumberland has persuaded me that the experience could assist your rehabilitation. I suggested a second member of staff, but Miss Cumberland has a point to prove.' Looking hard into our faces, she added, 'If any of you let me down, the consequences for the individual concerned will be very grave indeed – is that understood?'

'On behalf of my associates,' Ravi declared, 'I should like to thank you for giving us this unique opportunity to better ourselves, and rest assured, Miss Rice-Bird, your faith in us shall be richly rewarded.'

Ignoring Ravi, she directed her gaze at me. 'Allowing *you* to go, Mr King, is a serious risk.'

'I appreciate it,' I said.

We went up the walls that second night, crazy for Kalmasol – Ravi, Shelly and Archie cursing me and my no-dope dodge.

'First few days are always the worst,' I said. 'It'll get easier – trust me.'

Getting to sleep was a nightmare. We sat up cursing and laughing, playing dead each time Moses appeared. Then, out of nowhere – disaster. Ravi, moaning about his visits being suspended, was saying, 'How in God's name are we supposed to reform when we're cut off from our families?' when Archie attacked him with a chair, and Shelly and I had to drag him off and pin him on the floor.

'I'm sick of you rubbing my face in it – you all do it!' he accused, referring to all our family visits. In all his time at Dovedale he'd only ever received one surprise visitor, a soft-hearted teacher from his old school. 'I'll kill him, I swear!'

'Cool it, Archie, we'll get you through this,' I said.

'I'll kill you all and then meself – that'll teach you.'

'We should never have flushed his pills away,' said Shelly.

Archie crawled back into bed – buried himself under blankets. I patted Ravi on the back, swapped relieved sighs with Shelly and got into bed.

Moses looked in, flung his light about and went away.

Peace at last – or so I thought – and I was just drifting off when I *smelled* trouble. It was coming from one of Ravi's top drawers. I investigated. His Hindu holy book, permitted instead of a Bible, was smouldering. The hardback cover was intact, but tiny red sparks were nibbling away at the pages. Smothering the embers, I closed the drawer to cut the supply of oxygen and went over to Archie to confront him – and found him gone, covers thrown back, bed empty.

'Shelly? Trouble!' I hissed, trying in vain to shake him awake, and darted into the passage. My imagination ran riot – Archie stalking the corridors, determined to torch the building – Archie tearing through Strapps Wood, doing a Tony Trevino. Listening out, I could hear Moses chatting down below with the security guard. Peering over the banister, I could just make them out playing cricket in the entrance hall, a radiator the wicket. Wait a minute – the bathroom, I thought. Check the bathroom. I ran down the passage – paused to listen. Yes, someone was there, in the jacks, cursing under his breath. I went in and saw a figure sitting in the far corner, flicking a cigarette lighter on and off.

'Archie . . . ?'

He was waving the flame under one hand and then the other, wincing with pain, concentrating on his half-missing finger.

'That's crazy play, Archie.'

He laughed. I squatted near him.

'Lemme me try that,' I said, holding out my hands.

He pulled away – kept on burning himself.

'Archie, give it a rest, for Chrissake.'

'What do you care?'

'I do care, if you really wanna know.'

'You're such a gimp, King – nobody gives a monkey's. Don't you get it? It's dog-eat-dog.'

'Try it on me,' I said, holding up my palms.

He flashed the lighter at me – I didn't move. His shaking hand brought the flame closer and closer to my face. The lighter was running out of gas and burning low, but still I caught the sting and lashed out, seized Archie by the wrist and disarmed him. He fell back laughing – pressed his hands to the cold wall tiles. Then he wasn't laughing, he was banging his head on the wall.

'Whoa, Archie, leave those tiles alone!'

Slam – slam – slam – Archie smacking the wall with his head.

'C'mon, man' – putting my hands on him – 'that's enough.'

'Geddoff me!'

'Those hands need dressing.'

'What you talking about?' Parading his burned hands – 'This is normal – this is what I do – this is me without the meds!'

'You don't need meds, Archie, you need your talents recognized.'

'What, pickpocketing?'

'Absolutely – Olympic Gold for Archie Manzini!'

'You're a head case, you really are.'

'You don't need meds, Archie, you need mates, you need people like Alice, and all you do is reject people who wanna help you – it's crazy, man, you wanna get a new angle.'

'Drugs are my only mates, and you wanna take them away – thanks a lot, you're a real pal,' he said, writhing in pain.

'I'm sorry, Archie. I'm only trying to help.'

'Don't bother – I'm on my own. And it suits me fine.'

'I hear you, man, but those hands need attention.'

He looked at his grilled hands, living wounds in the dim light. He let me lightly take his elbow and lead him to a sink, where I ran a tap and watched while he dipped a hand into the flow and let out a squeal. I plugged the sink and held first one of his hands and then the other under water. He started sobbing, a mournful wail.

A shadow entered.

'Up to your old tricks again, Mr Manzini,' murmured Moses.

Archie started to pass out. Moses lifted him over his shoulder, carried him down to the office and unlocked the first aid box. Under stronger light Archie's hands didn't look as bad as I'd thought – more the venting of distress than dangerous self-harm. I watched Moses tenderly dress Archie's wounds.

I went to bed feeling bad. It was my fault Archie had freaked. And yet, I was right to want to help him, right to try and get him off the stuff – wasn't I?

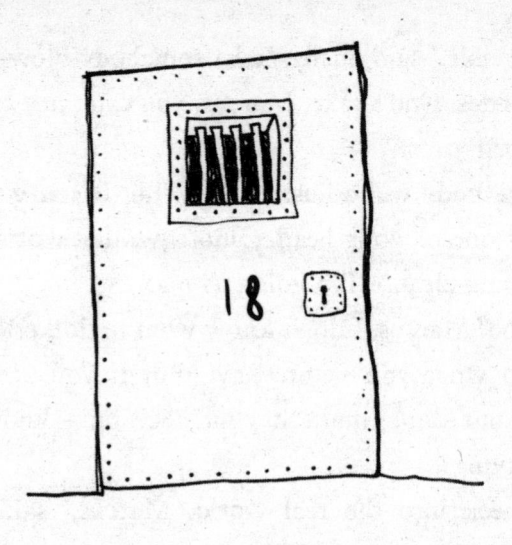

Getting Archie out of bed next morning was like waking a corpse. Shelly and I helped him to the bathroom – everyone looking at his bandages.

Back in the coop Shelly rounded on me – 'See what happens when you don't know what you're doing? They'll never let him out tomorrow in that condition.'

'What?' said Archie, tearing at his bandages with his teeth and flinging them in the bin. 'I'm going!'

'You're back on your drugs this morning,' Shelly insisted, pointing at him.

'Don't worry, Dr Petticoat, I can't wait.'

'Fifty p in the slagging box, Archie!' I said.

He told me to eff-off.

'How are you two this morning?' I asked.

'Distinctly wobbly,' said Ravi, 'and somewhat splendid!'

'Terrible,' said Shelly. 'Like somebody blow-torched my insides. God's sake, Marcus, you can't just come off this stuff.'

'The body will adjust,' I said. 'But if you wanna go doped out of your head tomorrow, that's up to you. I'm going clean – I'm going as *me*.'

'God, Marcus, I don't know what to do!' cried Ravi.

'Do what you want, Ravi. But if you are gonna take your dope, make it your decision – know what I'm saying?'

'Check into the real world, Marcus,' said Shelly. 'When you get a minute.'

I was really annoyed, convinced that Shelly and Ravi would duck out of our drug-free experiment, and that after being caught burning his hands, Archie wouldn't be let out at all. I was wrong. They simply upped Archie's meds – a pink and two blues to keep him docile. And as for Ravi and Shelly, they surprised me at breakfast, that day and the next, by joining me in my no-dope chewing-gum stunt, each of us pulling it off without a hitch.

Our spirits lifted – we were getting out for the day. I was going to get to the seaside without even having to do a runner! We travelled in Miss Wonderland's car, clean tracksuits, hands and faces scrubbed. It was rain-ing, and apart from Archie, who was pale and quiet, we were all singing, even Alice. Ravi sat in the front, booming out arias from Italian operas. The rest of us sat squished in the back, grinning and joking. What a gas! It was so great getting out, I didn't even mind being cooped up in a car. Alice drove with all the windows open just in case.

'Can we drive with the doors open an' all, miss?'

'No problem, Marcus.'

'How far's the airport, miss?' said Ravi.

'*What?*' said Archie.

'Don't tease him,' said Alice.

Beneath all the larking about I was focused on my escape plans, studying the landscape, the denseness of woodland, the absence of visible footpaths, the contrast of open wilderness and cover. I was now on my fourth day off Kalmasol, struggling but getting stronger. Another ten days or so and I expected to be fit and ready.

Miss took a few wrong turns – 'The story of my life!' she said – and the journey was more like two hours. Ravi dozed in his seatbelt, Archie picked his scabs, I hung out the window, feeling seasick, and Shelly painted his finger-nails a delicate lilac and applied matching eye shadow.

Alice smelled something – 'Shelly, what are you doing?'

'Don't you like them, miss?' he said, parading his nails.

'They're gorgeous – but how are we going to explain them?'

'I can't imagine disabled kids will care what colour my nails are.'

'It's not the kids I'm worried about.'

Crossing a bridge into a small border town, we

stopped for a leak at a mobile hut at the foot of a castle crawling with sightseers. Miss stretched her legs. Shelly disappeared. We waited for him back at the car.

'He looked so pretty, perhaps someone ran off with him!' said Ravi.

'Or beat him up,' said Archie.

'Thank you, lads,' said Alice, getting nervous.

Then, just as she was threatening to call the cops, up pops a pretty girl, swinging a shopping bag, and ducks into the back of the car –

'Skates on! We haven't got all day.'

Shelly had spotted an Oxfam shop and bought a sleek silk skirt, sequinned top and medium heel shoes, completing the makeover with dark-pink lipstick, earrings and a fetching pink beret. He-she looked amazingly cool and relaxed, straightening her skirt in the back seat.

'Bloody hell,' said Archie.

'My dear fellow, you look simply . . . ravishing!' said Ravi.

'For God's sake, Shelly,' said Alice as we drove on. 'How am I going to introduce you to the Principal?'

'As a girl.'

'Dovedale doesn't take girls.'

'I'm the exception!' declared Shelly. 'The authorities were stuck for a place, and Miss Rice-Bird, out of the kindness of her heart—'

'He'll need a new name,' said Archie brilliantly. 'A girl's name.'

'I think Shelly might just do,' I said.

'Where's your uniform, Shelly?'

'Relax, miss.' Shelly patted the shopping bag and broke into some old song – '*I'm just a girl who can't say no . . . !*'

'Forgive me, miss,' said Ravi. 'He's even prettier than you.'

'Definitely,' she agreed. 'But that's not saying much.'

'Nonsense! A certain someone finds you exceptionally attractive, don't you, Marcus?'

'We all do, miss.'

'Thank you – you've made my day.'

'Can we call you by your first name?' said Shelly.

'Just for today.'

'*Alice*,' I cried, 'what are you doing tonight?'

Nearing our destination, Shelly checked herself in a pocket mirror and Archie lit up a cig. Alice asked him to put it out – he ignored her. We all had a go at him, and when he carried on, Alice pulled over, switched off the engine and folded her arms. Good move. Archie took a final pull and flung the thing out the window.

'I want you all to enjoy today,' said Alice, driving on. 'I also want you to be bloody angels, all right?'

'Alice, you got any perfume I could borrow?' said Shelly.

We turned into a tunnel of trees dripping with rain. The place was called Runningdene – a new building in an old style overlooking the sea. A handful of disabled kids lived here. Others visited for assessment and therapy.

We were met at the entrance by Alice's friend Fiona, a young woman with hennaed hair and friendly Scots accent. She took us inside to meet Mr Gough, the boss, a lanky old bloke with specs round his neck and a moustache crying out for a trim. Alice tried placing herself in front of Shelly, but Mr Gough wanted to meet each of us in turn. When he got to Shelly, he popped his specs on.

'Goodness! I had no idea you took *gals*.'

'Bit of a surprise to me too,' said Alice.

'Well, I'm delighted to meet you and I trust you'll all have a dazzling day!'

The day took a bit of time to dazzle. After refreshments we were led to a room full of bean bags, mats and musical instruments, and introduced to our partners. Shelly was paired off with a black boy with cerebral palsy called Louis; Ravi with a road accident victim called Melanie; Archie with an autistic kid called Clive. I was paired off with a blind girl. The room was big, windows and door mercifully open.

The others were nervous all of a sudden, lost for what to do and say, each wishing he'd stayed home in cosy old Dovedale. Fiona and Alice did their best to jolly things along, but in the end it was every man for himself.

My partner was pale and silent. She sat on a window ledge, face angled to sky and birdsong, seeing nothing. Fiona touched her shoulder and murmured something about a visitor. The girl nodded – and kept on gazing blindly out the window, as though feeling the light. I looked at her, knowing she couldn't see me looking.

The others were all nearby in the big room, but I felt strangely alone with my blind partner. Even with open doors and windows, there was something oppressive about the place, but I couldn't put a finger on it.

'Hi . . . I'm Marcus.'

I thought for a moment she might be deaf as well, but at the sound of my voice she looked up, surprising me with the shyness and openness of her smile, as if somehow she was seeing me through my voice, not me physically, but me.

'Hi, Marcus.'

'Cool to meet you,' I said.

'Cool to meet *you* – I'm Shannon.'

She had a nice northern voice – soft but confident, catching your attention. Her hair was cut stylishly short with highlights. She had large, misty eyes – blind but beautiful – and thick dark eyebrows. She wore jeans, trainers and a short-sleeved T-shirt with the motto BUSINESS AS USUAL.

'What are you doing in Dovedale Hall?' she asked straight out.

'Good question—' I kind of laughed, embarrassed.

'You don't have to tell me, Marcus.'

Something in the way she said it made me want to.

'I kept running away from school – serial truant. I preferred the seashore.'

'They sent you away just for that?'

'Well, it's been going on since I was five. And you've got to throw in pretending to have left school to get odd jobs – and a bit of shoplifting when hungry. It's my own fault. Just never could stand being banged up with a million other kids, told what to do, what to learn and how – know what I'm saying?'

'I do.'

'Everyone in uniform being tested on the same work all over the country— You *do*?'

'I'm not like you, Marcus, I work hard in school, I have to, I want to – to keep up – but I know what you're saying.'

Silence. Surprisingly comfortable silence.

'What's it like in Dovedale?'

'Brilliant – golf courses, saunas, dry ski slope.'

She laughed, embarrassed. 'I get told off all the time for being too direct. Don't mind me.'

'No worries – I like it.'

I felt Fiona watching us. She and Alice were standing in the middle of the room, arms folded, observing everything. The lovely Shelly was hitting it off with Louis, his cerebral palsy partner. They were trying out some kind of nutty dance routine, Louis getting through a complicated series of jerky movements that looked impossible, but worked. Fiona was watching with interest. Louis obviously didn't boogie with everyone.

Ravi wasn't doing so well. His partner, Melanie, a chubby girl with pigtails, who was eighteen but looked twelve, sat in her wheelchair totally spaced. The accident must have blown her brains out. Ravi had tried everything, even tickling her.

Archie was having a ball. His autistic partner Clive was a live wire – grabbing things and putting them back – picking up the same objects over and over and replacing them in the same order. He had a surprising selection of keys on his belt, like a lunatic jailer; his overalls were packed with all kinds of door-locks and padlocks, and he was showing an amazed Archie how fast he could take a lock apart and put it back together again.

'You don't live here, do you, Shannon?'

'God no! I live at home with my mum.'

'Sorry, my turn to be too direct.'

'It's cool, Marcus. I get a lot of phoney crap from people. *She's blind so she must be an idiot.*'

'I can imagine.'

'You can?'

'Totally.'

'I come here once in a while for assessment and stuff, because the eyes are getting steadily worse and I'm having to learn to cope.'

'I'm sorry to hear it.'

'It's a drag, but it's not fatal. You OK, Marcus?'

She was amazingly perceptive.

'Do we have to stay in here, Shannon? It's hard to explain, but—'

'You don't have to. Let's go.'

She stood up – reaching for my shoulder. Linking her arm through mine, she started leading me across the room. Fiona reacted like a snake, but pretending to be cool.

'Shannon . . . ?' like, *Where are you going?*

'Just going for a walk, Fiona.'

'Where to?'

'I'm showing Marcus the sea.'

'I don't think that's a good idea.'

Shannon kept going, somehow following exit signs, relying on me to avoid obstacles.

'We'll be fine, Fiona, it's OK.'

'No, Shannon, it's not OK. And anyway, it's raining.'

'It's nearly stopped, the sun's coming out,' Shannon insisted, and I wondered how she knew, and still she kept going, with Fiona on our heels.

'As far as the fountain and no further, Shannon, you understand?'

Shannon pulled me out the back door into the open air.

She took my hand and led me across a playground.

'Aren't you cold?' I said, feeling the bite of a sea breeze.

'No, I love it.'

Her hand felt warm and strange. Steering from memory, she headed for a garden. 'There are steps around here somewhere.'

'This way a bit,' I said.

The steps were narrow – we pressed against each other going up. The garden didn't amount to much – a few sad flowerbeds and steel benches with holes in like on railway platforms. Shannon kicked off her shoes! Bare feet on damp flags. She felt her way towards a stone fountain, sat on the rim and took back her hand. The sun came out.

'You were right, Shannon.'

The water in the fountain was deep and murky and I was on edge in case she fell in, but she sat kicking and sunning her legs. She'd chosen to sit where the breeze blew spray from the fountain in her face.

Water was also coming from above – rain! She smiled and lifted her face to meet it. Raindrops gathered in her hair. Without looking towards me she said, 'Where are you from?'

'London – *ain't it obvious*!'

Her hand was on the move – found my head, my hair – stayed with my hair.

'Are you black?' she asked.

'Sort of.'

'Sort of?'

'Two-tone, if you know what I mean.'

'Cool.'

'Caramel complexion, red hair.'

'Red?'

'From my mum.'

She started feeling my face, its shape, then the nose, then, carefully, my eyes and mouth, sending shivers through me. Then she brought her other hand into play and with two hands found my arms and hands. She seemed particularly interested in my hands, turning them over, feeling the lines in my palms, making me tremble with the strangeness of her touch.

'You're going to live to a ripe old age, Marcus.'

'Can you tell?'

'You're going to marry young.'

'How young?'

'Eighteen.'

'*What?*'

'Loads of kids.'

'Really? How many?'

'Let me see . . . nine.'

'*Nine?*'

'Wait – *ten.*'

'You serious?'

'No!'

'You're messing!'

'What kind of music do you like, Marcus?'

'All kinds, but mostly I like making my own – you know, like grime? Eight-bar?'

'No-fake street stuff.'

'Right!'

'Your own MCing – that's so cool! I'd love to do that.'

'I'll show you – soon as I get out!'

'Shannon?' – Fiona calling.

Shannon ignored her. 'Do you do it all on a PC, Marcus?'

'Used to, but I've got my own crew now. We're called PleeztameetU and we were just starting to get noticed when I got Dovedaled.'

'When are they letting you out?'

'I wish I knew. I was ready to be released for good behaviour, but they found an excuse to pin another six months on me. Criminals and delinquents – no problem – but rebels with working brain cells . . .'

'Shannon! Will you come in now, please. It's raining!'

We got up and wandered back.

'Another six months sounds horrific, Marcus.'

'They sell themselves as a model institution committed to rehabilitation, and aren't we the lucky ones – but it's a prison, Shannon, with wilderness for walls, and drugs as instruments of control.'

'Drugs?'

'Everybody's on them. It's repression, not rehabilitation.'

'That's *abuse*.'

'Half the lads are depressed, scared out of their wits or suicidal.'

'Not surprised.'

'We stumbled on this UN report in the library, slamming the UK for running places like Dovedale.'

'It named Dovedale?'

'I wish.'

She stopped – laid a hand on my shoulder. 'How do you stand it, Marcus?'

'I don't know – you just do.'

Her hand found mine and squeezed it.

'I'm getting out, Shannon. It's the one thing I'm really good at. I'll keep running and running till I'm not a minor any more, and maybe then they'll leave me alone.'

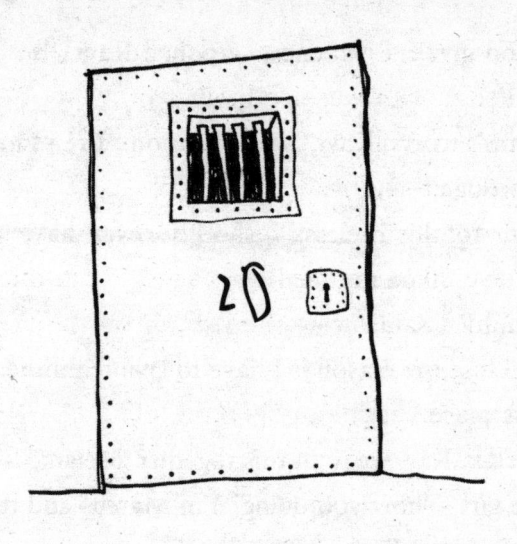

I hated going back indoors. Shannon wasn't too thrilled either and sat in the window, knees pulled up to her chin. I'd felt so free with her out there. I leaned on the wall beside her, the two of us hanging loose, not saying anything.

I caught Alice's eye; she smiled. Everyone was getting on with his partner, except old Ravi, who was getting agitated.

'Keep trying, Ravi,' said Fiona. 'You never know.'

I guessed Fiona was only saying that. Melanie probably hadn't flicked a switch in years, and Ravi was tearing his hair out, throwing longing looks towards the exit. I signalled him to bring Melanie over, and he nearly did a back-flip he was so relieved. Wheeled her over and parked her right next to me.

'God give me patience,' groaned Ravi, 'but make it quick!'

'Don't worry, Ravi,' said Shannon. 'Even Fiona can't get through.'

'I'm totally useless. I should never have come! I should've taken my meds!'

'Shhh!' I said.

'I'll lose my reason if I have to spend another minute in this place.'

'Relax, Rav, we're in this together. Melanie' – turning to the girl – 'how you doing? I'm Marcus and this is my mate Ravi the First of Rajisthan.'

I smiled imploringly at her. She looked right through me. I touched Shannon's hand. 'Does she ever get going?'

Shannon frowned, like, *Kind of*, and then shook her head – 'Nah.'

Shannon and I stayed close to Ravi over lunch, keeping him calm. We couldn't wait for the afternoon, when the weather was meant to pick up and we were supposed to hit the beach a couple of hundred metres away.

Then, right after lunch, someone noticed Archie and Clive were missing.

Fiona freaked. 'Everybody stay put while we raise the alarm!'

'Be good, all of you,' said Alice, and hurried after her.

We all stood around, waiting for someone to take a lead. I tried staying out of it. Didn't want any trouble so close to my appointment with freedom.

'I was looking forward to seeing the sea,' said Shelly.

'I was looking forward to taking you,' said Louis.

'I was looking forward to a bloody swim!' said Ravi.

We thought he was joking.

'What do you think, Shannon?' I asked impulsively.

Her sightless eyes sparkled. 'I say it's time to hit the beach!'

We couldn't get out fast enough, and Shelly, tripping in his heels on the slippery garden steps, twisted an ankle. He laughed it off, but was in pain and could barely stand. 'No worries,' said Louis, taking Shelly's arm. 'I'll take you to the nurse.'

We watched Shelly and Louis stumble like drunks back into the building. I carried on, arm in arm with Shannon. Ravi whooped with delight and began racing Melanie down a track built for wheelchairs.

'Whoa, Rav, take it easy!'

All at once – the open beach, sea and sky!

'Yo! Shannon – what a sight!'

'Isn't it great!'

Damn – I wished I hadn't said *sight*.

'It's OK, Marcus. I used to be able to see, so I *can* see it – I can see everything! Everything but you, because you're new!'

The track ended at the edge of the beach, which was wild and beautiful in a bleak kind of way, boulders and shingle and wolf-grey waves rushing to shore. The wind

smacked our faces. Ravi sang a manic aria and Melanie
– waking out of her trance – began to hum.

'Listen!' Ravi stopped dead. '*Listen!*'

Melanie was starting to sing loudly, out of tune, belt-
ing out nonsense.

'It's a miracle!' Ravi cried. 'The overture from *Il
Trovatore*!'

Dropping to one knee, Ravi grabbed Melanie's hands
and passionately sang along with her.

'What a wild duet, Ravi!' Shannon cried above the
wind. And then – 'Marcus? I understand you wanting
to run, I really do . . .'

'But what?'

'Don't you think you might be able to do better?'

Tensing up. 'Like what?'

'If Dovedale's that bad, shouldn't you be telling someone?'

'Don't you believe me?'

'I *do* believe you. That's why I'm wondering: have
you thought about blowing the whistle on that place?'

'Not really . . . until I read the article.'

'I dunno, Marcus, but maybe you've a duty.'

I stood gazing out to sea, knocked out by what she'd
said.

'Doesn't it smell great!' she cried.

'What?'

'The sea!'

'Yeah, it's amazing – it's all amazing!'

'Look, Marcus! *Marcus!*' Ravi was calling. 'Divine music and the sea-kissed breeze has roused Melanie from her slumber!'

'I know, Rav – you're brilliant, you're a superstar!'

'If only this blasted path went down to the sea!' he complained. 'Melanie, oh Melanie, what sayest thou I transport thy royal personage in person?' he cried. 'Come on, Lady Mel. Time to throw off life's tiresome shackles.'

Next thing I know, Ravi's taking his shoes and socks off . . . his sweatshirt and vest – all dumped on the stones!

'Ravi – take it easy.'

His trousers.

'Yo! Your Majesty, you might just wanna leave it at that!'

His *underpants*.

'Interesting move, Ravi.'

'What's he doing?' Shannon said.

'He's just taken his clothes off.'

'What . . . ?'

'Yup – not a stitch!'

She threw back her head and laughed!

'He's kneeling starkers at Melanie's feet – removing her shoes and socks . . .'

For a terrible moment I thought he was planning to take all her clothes off too.

'Come, Your Ladyship,' Ravi cried. 'Climb aboard!'

'Blimey, Shannon, she's leaning towards him – she can't wait.'

Melanie, paralysed from the waist down, clung round Ravi's neck with strong arms. And Ravi, wrapping her legs round his waist, hitched her up and trundled down the beach, sliding on stones.

'He's piggy-backing her down to the water, Shannon – *into* the water.'

'You serious?'

'This could get out of hand.'

'It's OK – they'll be fine.'

'You don't know what he's on – or rather *not* on.'

Ravi waded into the surf, singing loudly in Italian, giving it an extra oomph as each incoming wave broke over him.

'The water's up to his waist . . . That's far enough, Ravi!'

'She's laughing!' Shannon heard delightedly. 'Your friend Ravi's a natural!'

'Natural what?'

'No one's ever made Mel laugh like that.'

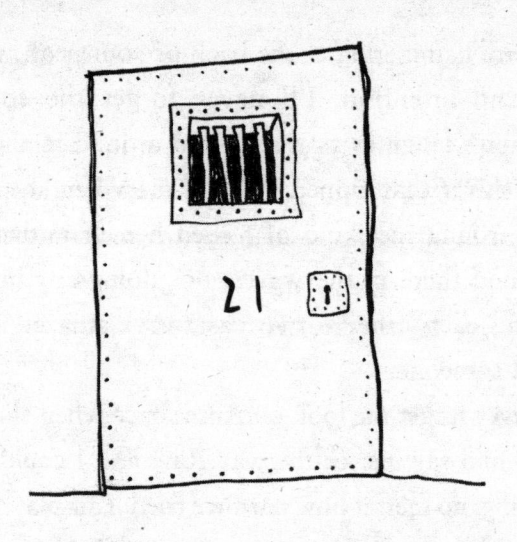

I'll never forget that day, the sight of Ravi wading into the water, bare bum and other unmentionables covered and then uncovered by the waves, Melanie screeching with laughter on his back.

Never forgot the joy on Shannon's face as she rolled up her jeans and yelled, 'C'mon, Marcus! Why should they have all the fun?'

She was feeling her way over the stones without me. I couldn't get my shoes and socks off fast enough. I should have rolled up my trousers but there wasn't time. Tore my blazer off and caught her up, tentatively took her arm – she seized my hand.

Into the freezing water we went, yelling at the wind. I knew it wasn't a good move giving my best trousers the full wash and spin, but there are moments you can't let go – they're too wild, too exciting, and though your fears are hammering at the back of your head, you pay them no attention. I'll never forget the sound of Shannon's laughter as we jumped around in the waves – the shiver that zipped through me when she put her arms around me, kind of folded herself into me, and we stood there in the waves, not doing anything, just holding each other – two castaways amazed to have found someone.

Never forget the look on Alice's face when she hit the beach and saw us, or the way Ravi and I couldn't stop laughing, no matter how hard we tried. Fair play to Alice, she tried desperately to cover for us, tried to make out it wasn't as bad as it looked. She was like a mum doing her best to pick up the mess after her darlings have wrecked a supermarket. Never forget Fiona's face when she saw Melanie and Shannon drenched head to toe – or Mr Gough's at the sight of Clive and Archie high up in the branches of an oak tree, puffing cigarettes and blowing smoke rings.

'You want me to go up, sir?' I offered.

'What? Don't you think two of them up there is enough?'

'They're *stuck*, sir. They can't get down.'

I climbed and reached out, but they were like two cats who'd had fun going up, and now couldn't even *look* down. They had to call the flipping fire brigade! Shannon and I were killing ourselves trying not to laugh.

Poor Alice was nearly in tears. Actually she was in

tears. Fiona stood with her arms folded and Mr Gough said he'd be straight on the blower to Miss Rice-Bird. They disappeared Shannon before we had a chance to say goodbye.

We drove back in high sprits, condemned men having a last laugh. I'd just met someone brilliant and beautiful – and lost her. I couldn't believe it.

The state of us! Shelly had washed off the make-up and was back in uniform, but with a strapped ankle. Archie's shirt and trousers were in tatters, and he'd managed to lose his sweatshirt. As for Ravi and me, we were comparatively respectable after our romp in the North Sea. Nearing Dovedale, we all fell silent. Not a whisper, just the cranky old engine and Alice tapping her nails on the wheel. The headlights felt their way along the avenue – picked out the familiar outline of Mr Strang on the front steps. All five of us took a deep breath. The Predator was smoking a thin cigar, his face expressionless.

'Miss Rice-Bird will see Miss Cumberland first.'

We waited in the corridor, facing the wall in the regulation position, listening. The Iceberg hardly knew where to begin. Alice did her best to defend us, saying each of us in his own way had taken great pains to look after his partner. We heard the Iceberg laugh in disbelief, heard her call Alice *reckless* and *irresponsible*.

My heart shook. We looked at each other.

The Iceberg saw us separately. I was last in. She was sitting behind her desk, eyes brilliant in a face of stone.

'Well, Mr King, congratulations.'

'I'm sorry about today, miss—'

'You've really surpassed yourself.'

'But it really wasn't as—'

'Your stupidity takes the breath away.'

'If only you could have seen—'

'Not to mention your lack of gratitude.'

'The joy on their—'

'And to think you gave me your word.'

'The supervisor was really impressed—'

'And that I was willing to trust you.'

'Your Dovedale boys actually did you proud—'

'Treachery's a word that springs to mind – I'm frankly speechless.'

She wasn't actually: she got up and started to pace, banging on without drawing breath. She had shown me kindness and consideration and I'd thrown it back in her face. She'd gone out on a limb for me and I'd violated her trust. It was unforgivable!

'What on earth goes on in your mind, young man? Didn't you think you were in deep enough water already? Oh, you think it's funny, do you?'

'No, miss – it's just, you know, *deep water*?'

'Drug-taking and violence – and now leading a blind girl into the sea! I had thought that you, Ravi and Sheldon possessed some small intelligence, some hidden seeds of redemption, but Mr Strang is right – I should have listened – you really are beyond salvation.'

'No, miss, believe me—'

'Which leaves me only one remaining option.' The Iceberg sat down triumphantly and started writing. 'I've done my best . . . there's nothing more I can do.'

My heart flickered, a moment's hope, picturing Laura Rice-Bird washing her hands of me, dropping me in person at the station.

'Let Mr Strang see what he can do,' she said, opening her bag and taking out her lipstick.

I stood gazing at her, hands behind my back.

'I hope you like it here, Mr King,' she said, touching up her lips, 'because you're going to be with us for a very long time.'

Alice was waiting outside to escort me upstairs.

'You're in trouble, aren't you?' I said.

She smiled – she was in shock. 'I'm to be gone by morning.'

The coop was hushed. The others had just had six-month extensions hammered onto their sentences. Me, I'd just had *a very long time* added to mine, and I had a feeling a very long time meant even longer than six months. I was already on another six months and had served barely two weeks of it. I could still be here a year from now.

They were all in pyjamas, getting into bed. Alice sent me to brush my teeth. When I returned, the place was dark and still, the night sky dying down behind Alice in the window. I got into bed.

'I managed to wring one concession out of her,' she said. 'To let me say goodbye.'

My heart dropped like a stone down a bottomless well. I glanced at the others: Shelly lying back, hands behind his head, staring at the ceiling; Ravi sitting up, covers pulled up over his chin with just his eyes peeking; Archie lying with his head stuffed under his pillow.

'I don't blame any of you, it was my fault. You were wonderful with your partners – I'm proud of you. Fiona admitted she'd never seen Louis, Clive or Shannon so excited and happy. And when I pressed her, she agreed she'd never seen Melanie – soaked to the skin and shivering – looking so alive. Your methods were somewhat unorthodox, but . . .'

She caught her breath. 'I would've liked to continue teaching you until they find a replacement, but . . . you can see her point.'

With that she kissed each of us in turn on the forehead and left.

I lay on my bed, heart pounding. Our champion and guardian angel was gone. Somebody's suppressed sobs disturbed the awful stillness. After a time I got up and looked out at the cold moon, picturing Alice moving between our classroom and the staff room, collecting her things. Then I heard her engine start up, shattering the silence. You couldn't see the car park from our window, only her lights brushing the trees as she drove away.

I got into bed and lay in a fever of rage and guilt – and then a smile entered my heart, recalling Alice's reckless faith in us, which – even in defeat – remained unshaken.

You were wonderful with your partners – I'm proud of you.

I remembered Shannon . . . or a sudden sickness gripped me and I realized it was Shannon I was thinking about – reliving her laughter, that moment together in the waves, the thought of never seeing her again. Losing her was a knife in the belly – my guts fed to the gulls.

I've got to *do* something, I thought, and scrambled about for pen and paper.

Incoming letters weren't touched, but outgoing ones were liable to be plucked from the post box and read – like athletes and soccer stars randomly picked for dope tests – and returned to us in shreds. So what were my options? Risk the post box, or approach a whip I could trust. But now that Alice was gone, who could I trust? No one – except perhaps Mr Trust himself.

I sat on my bed, staring into space. If ever I'd harboured any doubts about escaping from Dovedale, they were blown away. What had happened at Runningdene wasn't all bad – some of it was fantastic, but the people who ran Dovedale seemed determined to see good as bad, creative as disruptive.

A very long time sounded like the rest of my life and

I wasn't going to wait around. I sat there, heart beating, nailing down my plans. It was now mid August. My body was slowly coming back and I reckoned on one, maybe two more Kalmasol-free weeks before I was fit enough to escape – end of the month or the beginning of September. Shannon had got me thinking – *You might be able to do better . . . have you thought about blowing the whistle on that place?* She was right, I'd only been thinking of me. I needed to talk to her, needed to see her.

I started a letter by the light of the moon, hoping someone would read it to her:

Yo, Shannon, it's me!

It was brilliant meeting you. You're amazing and beautiful. Why did it have to end such a mess? Why did they have to get it all so wrong? I got to talk to you about you know what – my DUTY. Write back quick – and let me have your address.

Stay cool.

Marcus

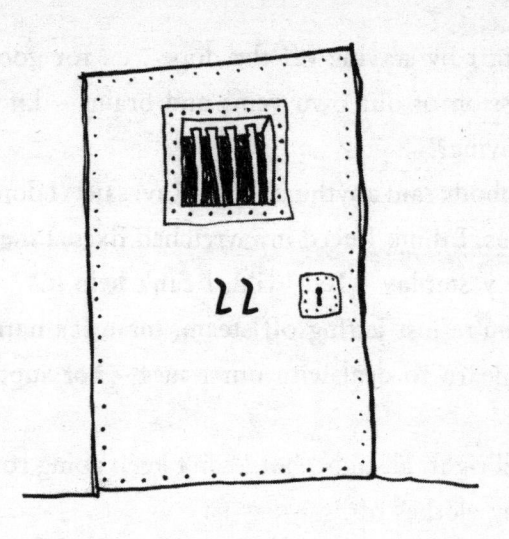

Next morning, we braced ourselves for the back-lash, but it was the Predator's day off.

'Thank God for small mercies!' shivered Ravi, manic without the meds.

My coopmates were pale with shock: six more months to face, 180 extra days in Dovedale, all for getting a little carried away at Runningdene, for putting smiles on faces. I was the only one not in shock, because I was taking things into my own hands. Escape was no longer an ambition – it was crucial.

No one spoke as we got washed – they couldn't even look at themselves in the mirror. We were getting dressed for breakfast when I broke the silence.

'Look, I know we're all hurting, but we gotta fight this. Any wrong we did yesterday was nothing next to the good. Reaction's been over the top and unfair. We can start by staying off the dope . . . for good. Keep possession of our own veins and brains – know what I'm saying?'

Nobody said anything. Then Ravi said, 'I don't know, Marcus, I think I need my wretched fixes. I mean, look at me yesterday – I go wild, I can't help it.'

'You're just letting off steam, man. It's natural. We gotta learn to deal with our issues – not suppress the stress!'

'All right, all right, but I can't keep going round taking my clothes off.'

'There's worse things, Rav, than taking your clothes off.'

'And I still have to survive six more months – oh my God, I can't believe it.'

'That's just my point, Ravi. Survival's not enough. To stay true to ourselves we've gotta resist, say, *No, we're not having this!* Even if we do it subtly, so they don't notice. For our own dignity.'

'Intellectually, yes, Marcus, I agree entirely, but practically speaking – my God . . .'

'You're all mouth, Marcus,' said Shelly. 'I've watched you, you've been close to the edge often enough, you could crack any time. Face it, we need the dope.'

'Tell me about it!' said Archie, shaking as he waited for his fix.

'Without the Kalmasol we'll keep on doing crazy things,' Shelly said. 'So let's just drop it, Marcus, all right?'

'Wait a sec, wait a sec,' I said. 'We've survived this far by pulling together. Strang's gonna come after us, and we'll need clear heads to stick together. United we stand, divided we—'

'Rubbish,' snapped Shelly, pointing a finger at me. 'I'm tired of listening to you. If we'd taken our dope, we'd have kept our heads and got through Runningdene without the extra six months – six months! I don't know about you, but I'd quite like to make it out of here before the next millennium.'

'He's right, Marcus – it's all gone too far,' said Ravi. 'If we really behave for the next couple of months, maybe the Iceberg will reconsider – what do you think, Shelly? Cut it to three months for good behaviour. So I say we should do the *opposite* of fight. We should take our medicine and knuckle down. You can't fight these people, they hold all the cards.'

'Yeah! And you better not try and stop us' – Archie's turn to aim a finger at me – 'I'm warning you.'

I looked at them in wonder. They looked at me in hate.

'You still don't get it, do you, Marcus?' said Shelly. 'So let me make it simple for you. *Obedient* we survive – *defiant* we fall.'

I looked away, shaken. We who had started out enemies and had gradually pulled together were coming apart again, and it really upset me. I felt like throwing something out the window – like throwing *them* out the window. My heart beat sickeningly, the thought of all resistance to Dovedale extinguished. A clean sweep for the forces of darkness.

'You're right,' I said. 'You're all absolutely right.'

They seemed surprised at this, and carried on dressing.

'We should have taken our dope and played by the rules,' I went on, looking out at the hills. 'Shelly and Louis could have sat playing Snap . . . Archie could have picked his nose while Clive picked his locks . . . Ravi could have twiddled his thumbs and clock-watched while Melanie stared into space . . . and I could have made small talk with my blind partner.'

Nobody said anything. I turned and looked at them.

'It was a great day yesterday . . . and you all wanna make out it was a tragedy? It wasn't a tragedy for me – it was brilliant. And you know what? Even if Shannon and I hadn't hit it off, I'd still say it was a bit special seeing Clive and Archie plucked out of that tree shaking with laughter, and Louis jiving with Shelly, and Shelly looking happy and beautiful, and Melanie shrieking for joy on Ravi's bare back. I'll never forget it long as I live.'

Shelly's eyes were welling up. But I wasn't finished.

'You boneheads might wanna bury yesterday – I don't. We brought light and joy to those guys, but if you wanna look on the dark side, I pity you. Take your punishment and your medicine and spend the rest of your sentences doped and submissive – the rest of your *lives* submissive, because trust me, if you're willing to surrender here, it'll become a habit you won't be able to kick. Once a puppet, always a puppet.'

I didn't know what I was saying – it all just tumbled out.

'We were *free* yesterday, we were alive and buzzing, and man, we were good! We were *awesome*! We were good without knowing how, without training and without drugs. Go on, all of you, knock on Strang's door and hold out your wrists so he can snap the handcuffs on – you'll feel much better. Why bother staying free when it's so much easier in chains?'

I didn't mean to hurt anybody . . . or maybe I did. I expected them to hate me, and maybe they did. I didn't care what they thought, I was too upset. All I saw was Archie squinting weirdly at me and cracking his fingers; Ravi trying to go about his business as usual; Shelly gazing at me with big wounded eyes.

I looked away, feelings of hopelessness growing as I realized we'd used up all the chewing gum and I'd be joining the dope queue any minute. There was no escaping the dope queue – every name got ticked off. I started to panic. *I'm not taking that stuff – I can't, I won't!*

On the way to breakfast, I nicked a bit of Blu-Tack off a notice board and chewed it as I joined the queue. When it got to my turn, I didn't bother returning Doughnut's cheery, 'Morning, Malcolm!' – I wasn't in the mood. When he gave me my pills I tongue-poked them into the putty behind my front teeth, and showed when he said show. It didn't work. It all came away and I swallowed the Blu-Tack along with the pills.

'I'm bursting!' I told a duty whip, and ran to the jacks, stuck a finger down my throat and puked it all up.

Under the suspicious gaze of the whip I returned to my table, where something was up. Word had spread fast – Skinny Hitler and Strangeboy Bland were sniggering at us; the whips were sharing a laugh. My coopmates stuck to their porridge, mortified. Moments later, the Iceberg appeared all in black, hair scraped back tighter than ever, eyes electric. The hall hushed.

'As soon as you've brushed your teeth and collected your school bags, you're all to proceed directly to the great hall.'

With that, she strode out again, and I pushed away my porridge.

Thirty minutes later we joined everyone in the hall. We sat cross-legged on the floor like primary kids, whips on chairs at the back. I remembered the motto in the Iceberg's office promising that Dovedale Hall was dedicated to the reform and rehabilitation of troubled boys, in order to return them to the community as useful citizens. If you believe that, I thought, you'll believe anything. It should have read: *Dovedale Hall is dedicated to breaking rebel spirits in order to turn them into zombies.*

'I need more gum,' I whispered to Archie.

'It'll cost ya.'

The Iceberg appeared. She went straight for the jugular.

'Barnicote, Sharma, Manzini and King – out to the front.'

All eyes on us as we went up and turned to face the smirking mob.

'Dovedale Hall offers young offenders the best chance of reform and rehabilitation of any equivalent institution in England . . . but it's entirely up to each of you whether or not you wish to make the best of it. These four delinquents clearly don't. Entrusted with a special day out to a renowned institution for disabled young people, they ran amok, betraying my trust and disgracing the good name of Dovedale. Their behaviour has regrettably led to the dismissal of Miss Cumberland, a well-meaning teacher who mistakenly put her faith in these four fools. I am cancelling all their privileges and visits under further notice, and I hardly need tell you that they are going to find life here pretty unpleasant from now on. Let that be a lesson to you all.'

On the way out we were mercilessly teased by jostling slogs, each of us responding in his own way – Shelly head high, Ravi head low, Archie hissing like a cat. As for me, when Skinny Hitler shouldered me into a radiator with the words, 'Noodle Head's so desperate, he has to chase blind girls!' I looked him in the eye and smiled, vowing somehow, when the opportunity presented itself, to get even.

At lunch time I slipped away, and sticking close to high hedges hurried down the lane, past Mr Strang's cottage and onwards until I reached a small field shielded by trees where Moses were said to camp out. There it was, a mobile home surrounded by flowers and vegetables neatly staked and tied. Pushing open the gate, I knocked on the door. And knocked again. A face appeared at a curtain. He was on night shifts and opened the door in his pyjamas.

'Sorry to disturb you, Mr Trust . . . bit of an emergency.'

'Heaven help us, what?'

'It's all right, it's nothing like that. I'm sorry, it's . . . just a favour.'

'Favour?'

'I shouldn't be asking you, but I need a letter posted.'

His shaved head tilted so far sideways to study me, I thought it might roll off his neck and flatten his tomatoes.

'You better come inside.'

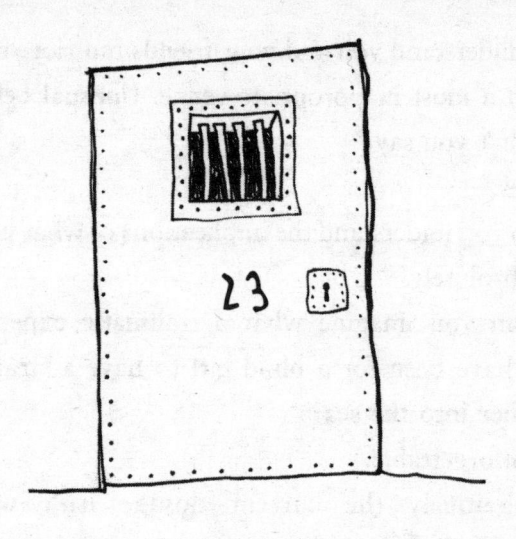

All that week, our lessons were taken in turns by the Iceberg herself and Mr Strang, making us work in absolute silence. Each time I looked up, I remembered Alice – how much she'd cared about us and risked for us, and how much we'd lost. I wanted to share these feelings with my coopmates – but suspected I'd lost them too.

Candidates for her job were shown into our little classroom. 'These are our little charmers,' the Iceberg said, and the bloke or woman gazed at us, and we gazed back, praying it'd be this one or that one, but definitely not *that* one.

One by one we were called out to see Dr Doughnut in his office. He was at the sink, humming as he washed his hands and dried them – and washed and dried them again. Then he sat at his desk, arranged a couple of pens precisely parallel and looked up.

'I understand you and your friends ran riot yesterday, and in a most inappropriate venue. Unusual behaviour, wouldn't you say?'

'Yes.'

'So you understand the implications of what you did?'

'Absolutely.'

'Can you imagine what a traumatic experience it must have been for a blind girl to have a strange boy drag her into the sea?'

'Unforgettable.'

'Obviously the current dosage isn't working, Malcolm. I'm prescribing a course of Kalmasol-XL4,' he said, writing it down.

A shiver went through me. 'That's pretty heavy ammunition, Doc.'

'Keep this up, young man, and you'll stay on it.'

'Go for it, Doc. Quicker we knock this thing on the head the better.'

At lunch break, Archie found me leaning on a wall in the yard. He sidled up beside me, and while we chatted about this and that, he fingered me the chewing gum – I fingered him the dough.

'Thanks, Archie. I really appreciate it.'

He kind of shrugged, resisting the smallest intimacy.

'I'll need more,' I said. 'A regular supply.'

'You're banging yer head, mate. Do yerself a favour and take the stuff.'

'No thanks, Archie. Me, I want a clear head and clean bloodstream. I want salmon leaping in my veins, my brain sharp as a blade, my legs capable of marathons.'

'You're mad, you are.'

I was tempted to let him in on my plans – show him I trusted him, even if I didn't.

'Last thing *I* want, Marco, is a clear head.'

The following day the Predator took our coop apart. He found my homemade bookmark – concealing the UN article – turned it over in his hand and sniffed it. He was suddenly more interested in the photo of my parents. Dismantling the frame, he looked for a second hidden photo and was disappointed.

I looked him in the eye – he gave me five hundred lines.

He found the secret hiding place where Shelly kept his make-up, and made him start his thousand lines in lipstick. He found a tiny feather under Ravi's bed and made him get down on all fours and sweep his area with it. He found a cigarette inside one of Archie's shoes and made him eat it.

Wearing a hollow smile, he set about making our lives hell. Every morning began one hour earlier – 5.30 a.m. – with a cold bath. He stood, arms folded, while we climbed in and sank up to our necks in freezing water for sixty seconds. Any attempt to sit up sooner, and we had to repeat it. The first time I went under, I thought my heart would explode out of my chest wall. Ravi screamed every time; Archie gurgled like a man in his death throes. Only Shelly underwent his morning torture without a murmur. The Predator observed us closely, making notes in a little book like a scientist. After our swim, it was tracksuits and trainers and round the rugby field twenty times – ten for Ravi. Anyone who failed to lap Ravi at least five times missed breakfast. After breakfast, another twenty laps as usual.

Then Mr Strang introduced us to wood-clearing, normally reserved as a punishment for senior slogs. After lunch every day – apart from Sunday – a whip marched us in single file through Strapps Wood to a wild overgrown area called The Buckle, about the size of ten football pitches and consisting of a mad mix of trees, shrubs and leg-catching brambles. We worked from two till six, using secateurs, shears and pruning saws to take out dead branches and clear the ground, leaving any promising saplings. After fifteen minutes our muscles cried out – another fifteen and we felt physically sick. At the end of every hour we were allowed five minutes to collapse, gulp water and take a leak behind a tree. Biscuits were doled out after two hours. Then the trudge back to Dovedale like prisoners on a death march, scratched, aching and blistered.

When the Predator was on we worked in silence. Wearing shades and wellies, but still in his suit, he sat on a tree stump reading the paper, looking up now and then to blow his hay-fevered nose. Anyone caught slacking was sent to bed without supper – a virtual death sentence for Ravi.

When the Predator wasn't barking at us – 'King, you cretin, you've missed those nettles! . . . Manzini, you ninny, it's only a wasp, not a sabre-toothed tiger!' – we worked to the sounds of shears snapping, secateurs snipping, saws screeching in dead wood, rain tapping leaves, the shriek of a startled pheasant. Strang never let up and the pain never let up – and yet it felt good sweating in the sun and rain, rescuing saplings from murderous brambles, freezing when a butterfly landed on me, or a dragonfly paused on a stem close enough to get a good look at its huge eyes and dazzling colours. Everything smelled wonderful. As more days went by without Kalmasol, my drug-dazed senses were starting to come alive again. The colours were stupendous. As I worked I was driven on by three thoughts: I'm getting out of here shortly; all this work is making me fitter for the escape; I'm gonna see Shannon again.

The more I got used to the work, the more I loved the hush of the woods, the smell, the company of trees. The only sound that spoiled it was old Strang snuffling and blowing his hooter. One time, returning to Dovedale at dusk after an extended session for slacking, we surprised a fox drinking from a ditch, a sleek red creature which looked up, startled, then plunged into the undergrowth and vanished. That's me, I thought, just watch me!

Harry Headcase supervised some afternoons and knew a bit about nature, and when he was in the mood he'd tell us that this flower was a Forget-Me-Not or a Yellow Pimpernel, and this butterfly a Small Tortoiseshell or Common Blue. The Predator hated the woods. When I once broke the silence with: 'Sir, any idea what that tree's called?' he lowered his paper and said, 'Never mind the blasted tree, Mr King. Five hundred lines – *I must remember to put my hand up.*'

I looked at him, wondering what made him tick.

Sometimes, for no apparent reason, he made us run all the way back to Dovedale, smacking the side of his boots with a stick to hurry us along. He had us where he wanted us, under his heel.

Old Moses supervised sometimes. He always started out strict, but softened in the sun. One hot afternoon, during the mid-session bickie break, we begged for five extra minutes' rest and he shrugged and gave in. Ravi collapsed on the ground, and the rest of us climbed into shady trees. Moses perched on a stump and closed his eyes. Bees droned, blissful minutes went by, none of us heard a jeep stalking through the wood. We lounged in cool trees, midges drawn to our sweat, not a care in the world.

Sunlight flashed on a moving windscreen, the jeep lurched into the clearing. Out sprang the Predator – 'Stay where you are!'

Old Moses kind of screwed up his face, like the

Almighty himself had caught him dozing on the job. The Predator stepped forward triumphantly, 'Well, well! Messrs King, Barnicote and Manzini taking their ease in the trees like so many degenerate monkeys, and Mr Sharma reclining on the floor like a vagabond. What happened to your time-keeping, Mr Trust? Break should be long over.'

Old Moses scratched his neck. 'It's a hot day, Mr Strang.'

'Leave it to me if it's too uncomfortable for you,' said the Predator, dismissing him with a flick of the wrist.

Off wandered Moses with his tail between his legs. The Predator lined us up and said, 'Now, gentlemen, I think we'd better compensate for lost time, don't you?'

He kept us working till after nine o'clock, or so I guessed from the light draining through the trees. By the time he herded us home like sheep in front of his tooting jeep, the wood was eerily quiet, the moon hung in the trees and a couple of bats zipped back and forth in the gloom, scaring Ravi out of his wits. Dry bread and water, and straight to bed.

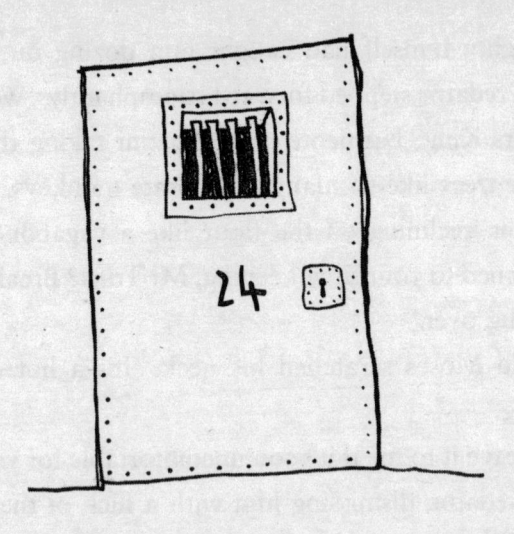

Night after night we'd fall asleep exhausted – and were still exhausted when the alarm blasted us awake next morning, ripping us from our beds like nails from wood. Only Shelly made it to the bathroom in the regulation sixty seconds, but old Moses generally looked away, a lenient shepherd with his tragic flock.

Everything was done in a virtual trance: cold baths and the Kalmasol queue; twenty laps of the pitch before and after breakfast; making beds and tidying areas. I was the only one pulling the no-dope stunt, the only one still suffering withdrawals – headaches and dizzy spells, less with every passing day.

Sleepwalking to class one morning, we found a stranger waiting. Our spirits shrank. He was tall and grim – craggy face and bushy eyebrows, a seasoned disciplinarian. He stood there, hands behind his back, regarding us with unconcealed loathing. Pre-emptive strike was his method – all-out war before we'd even sat down. His name was Mr Kyte, and looking into his eyes, we knew we'd met our match. This crusty old despot was the total opposite of our Alice – the triumph of darkness over light. Everything about him was dry, cold and angry. His eyes detected evil – his mind computed repression. From now on we'd need permission to breathe.

'When I call your name, you stand up and reply, *Yes, sir!* Barnicote?'

When it came to my turn, I rose slowly and said, 'Pardon me, sir, my name's Marcus and I have a – how shall I put it? – a fear of closed doors. My teachers generally leave it open . . . if you don't mind?'

'Don't be ridiculous. Answer your name – King?'

I looked away, gathering myself. 'Sorry, sir, but Miss Cumberland used to call us by our first names, and like I said, mine's Marcus.'

His eyes narrowed. 'You don't waste time, do you, Mr King?' he said, stepping right up to where I was standing. 'I was told to expect trouble, but I'm warning you, young man, I've taught and tamed boys a lot tougher than you.'

'Relax, Mr Kyte, you're making me nervous, you're making everybody nervous. We're not in the army here.'

His eyes bulged. 'Right, into the corner facing the wall – move!'

'I don't think so, sir.'

He reacted quickly for an old geezer – seized me by the arm and would have dragged me to the wall, only I grabbed his wrist and removed his hand. My strength surprised him.

'Why don't we sit down and discuss this, sir?'

'Let go of me!'

'We're not kids, Mr Kyte – we like a little respect.'

'I'm warning you!'

Still gripping his wrist, I rapped into his face:

> 'Hey, Mr Kyte,
> You're pretty uncool,
> You coulda had a smoother
> First day in school . . .'

'I'll count to three,' he said. 'One – two—'

> 'But you had to act tough,
> When you ain't tough enough,
> And now this fool
> Is gonna call your bluff—'

'Security!' he yelled. 'Security!'

'No need, guv,' I smiled, releasing him. 'Everything's cool.'

Someone arriving – Harry Headcase. The relief on Mr Kyte's face!

'Ah, Mr Ledpace! Would you mind escorting this violent individual to Mr Strang. If he's not there, make him wait outside – much appreciated.'

My classmates' shook their heads. I walked out without a second glance, the heat of Harry's eyes on my back.

'You don't learn, do you, lad?'

I was nervous. The prospect of mixing it with Mr Strang again turned my stomach. But I regretted nothing. I was sticking by my philosophy. Don't get pushed around – hit back.

Old Harry ushered me past classrooms where luckless teachers were locked in futile conflict with restless pupils, and knocked on the Predator's door. Knocked again – no answer.

'You're in luck, Mr King – for now. Wait in the regulation position.' He starting walking off, stopped and came back. 'I thought you were a bright lad, but arrogance and disrespect are second nature to you, King, aren't they?'

'It's funny, sir, but I always think of respect as a two-way street.'

He looked at me and let out a weary sigh. 'Look, Marcus, I don't enjoy seeing you lads suffer. But when you're released from here, I want you to leave a better person, more focused, more balanced. That's why I'm hard on you. You need discipline, son, can't you see that? Like a boy needs air, water and food, he needs *discipline* – you follow?'

We stood gazing at each other. He looked kind of desperate, and I wanted to tell him what old Moses had said about beaten dogs, and how boys need gentleness too, and love.

'Thank you, sir,' I said.

'Now stand up straight, there's a good lad,' he said gently, patted me on the shoulder and went on his way.

I stood, eyes closed, resting my brow against the wall. I was tired, I was weary of the fight. Without thinking, I tried the door, and it opened. Old Strang usually locked it, but for some reason it wasn't locked that day, like it was fate. I looked in, half expecting him to be sitting there waiting for me. But all was quiet and I went in, leaving the door fractionally ajar so I could hear.

Heart pounding – alone in the Predator's lair.

I'd been in here before, usually to deliver a million lines of *I must not do this or that* – and to leave with a furious lecture ringing in my ears. His office had a desk big as a barge and shelves of books with titles like *The Faulty Gene* and *The Roots of Deviancy*. More interesting was the door marked STRICTLY PRIVATE, the cupboard that sparked so many sinister rumours, where not even the cleaners were allowed.

A wave of dizziness hit me – *Damn! I'm not ready to run yet*, I thought, and caught myself against the Predator's desk, sat down in his black leather throne.

'*Stand up straight, you horrible creature!*' I murmured.

'You're a disgrace to your uniform, your underwear and the entire human race, and it'd give me great pleasure to . . .'

My eye wandered to the forbidden door. What if it concealed compromising material I could use against Dovedale?

The desk had three chunky drawers to one side. I opened the top drawer and was amazed to find a loaded pistol and ammunition. Actually there was nothing but pens, paperclips and stacks of A4. I tried the middle drawer. Aha! Handcuffs and electrodes. No, just the Predator's personal medicine store of painkillers, cough mixtures, hay-fever remedies. I opened the bottom drawer. It was divided into two parts: one contained chequebooks and cash, the other a big bunch of keys. I pricked my ears: no sound in the corridor. The cash didn't interest me – I'd be prime suspect anyway – but what about those keys?

I got up and approached the private door, tried every Yale-type key until one went in and turned. Still the door resisted, and I looked again and saw a second Chubb-type lock at thigh-level. I started again until I found a key that fitted and turned first the Chubb and then the Yale. Listening out, I went in, and saw at once that it wasn't a cupboard, but a large wood-panelled room. The window was curtained off, the air stale.

Feeling for the light switch, I blinked in surprise. The room was floodlit from below – search lights picked out scores of planes hanging on threads from a false ceiling hung with stars – plastic homemade kits suspended in flight, moving slightly in the draught from the door; all kinds of planes: prototypes and Spitfires, Second World War bombers and more recent models – Korea or Vietnam, I wouldn't know – and up-to-the-minute attack helicopters and Stealth fighters, all war planes and all displaying RAF or USAF markings.

To one side stood a trestle table cluttered with construction materials – craft knives, glues and paint, magnifying glass. Beside it an armchair, not like the macho job in the office, but a soft, rounded one with a footstool for relaxation. Alongside it a small table jumbled with unwashed coffee cups and glasses, an ashtray of twisted cigar butts, a half bottle of whisky. And something else – a small control panel. I reached and flicked a switch – and all the searchlights came to life, swaying this way and that in pursuit of prey. I tried another switch and a soundtrack clicked on – eerily realistic sirens, anti-aircraft guns, the drone of bombers. Amazing.

Enough of that! I thought, flicked the switches back off, turned to go and went, *Whoa! What's that? It can't be!* I stood beneath a swooping biplane, and there in the cockpit, taking on the world single-handed, was my fighter-pilot mouse, the one Clem had given me and Mr Strang had confiscated long ago with something like, *How old are you, for goodness' sake?*

'Yo! Email, what you doing here?'

My voice echoed in the hollow room. I stopped and listened, and reached up to reclaim my property, and then thought better of it. Email looked pretty cool as a First World War fighter ace – why steal his glory?

Noises! Voices! It was Mr Strang somewhere near, letting rip. Leaving Email to his adventures, I backed out of the room, switching off the lights, and softly closed the door. Out in the corridor the Predator was roaring at a bunch of slogs who were hotly denying some foul deed.

'Get in there and line up!' he shouted, and before my eyes, half a dozen senior slogs barged into the office, followed by the man himself, white with rage. 'Because I assure you, gentlemen, nobody is going anywhere until the reprobates who upended Miss Rice-Bird's window-boxes come clean.'

As the agitated slogs jostled into a line, I shuffled myself in among them.

'You can stand here all day – it's no skin off my—' He stopped suddenly. 'What are *you* doing here?' He was staring at me.

'Mr Kyte sent me.'

'Who?'

'The new teacher.'

'What for?'

'Singing out of tune, sir.'

Vandals snickered.

'Get back to class! I'll deal with you later.'

I left the office high with nerves. I should have been chuffed to be the first person to get behind Mr Strang's private door, but I was disappointed. I'd been hoping to find something damning, but the Predator's private hobby was hardly going to sink Dovedale. Worse, I now became aware of something heavy jingling in my pocket. No! His keys. I couldn't believe it! Flattening myself against a wall, I tried to think. What the hell do I do with his friggin' keys?

My mind was blank. I saw myself spending the next forty years in custody, coming out in my fifties to hug my grey-haired folks and middle-aged sister.

Then, as I leaned against the wall racking my brains – an idea! Leave the keys on the ground by the Predator's car – he'll think he dropped them. Wait a sec. A more interesting plan crawled out of a drain. Two birds with one bunch of keys – save myself and bury Skinny Hitler, as promised. Ears and eyes peeled, I went up to the top floor and found the coop Skinny Hitler shared with Strangeboy Bland and two other toffs.

Noodle Head's so desperate, he has to chase blind girls, I recalled as I shoved the keys under Skinny's mattress, and returned to class.

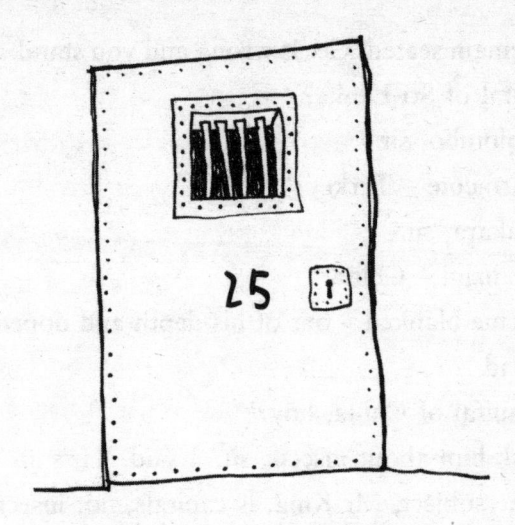

Dear Alice, how we missed her! Mr Kyte's voice was like a road drill. We wilted in our seats. He made lessons so boring, an intravenous caffeine drip wouldn't have kept us awake. Worst of all, the door was closed and I was shaking and grinding my teeth.

'Keep still, boy – what's the matter with you?'

Shelly put his hand up. 'Sir, he's not being awkward, he has a genuine dread of closed doors – particularly classroom doors.'

'Especially when the teacher's a fascist,' murmured Ravi.

'Then he'd better make an appointment to see the doctor!'

I knew he was going to say that.

'Right, hands on desks, backs straight – last night's homework, geography, world capitals. Get it right and you remain seated. Get it wrong and you stand. Sharma – capital of Sri Lanka?'

'Colombo, sir.'

'Barnicote – Turkey?'

'Ankara, sir.'

'Manzini – China?'

Archie blanked – out of his depth and doped out of his head.

'Capital of China, boy?'

'Ask him about insects, sir,' I said. 'He's an expert.'

'The subject, Mr King, is capitals, not insects.'

'With respect, Mr Kyte, Archie's not interested in capitals, he's interested in insects.'

'I'm not here to indulge your interests, Mr King, I'm here to make you boys learn.'

'Then you'll fail, Mr Kyte, because you've got to be interested to learn.'

In the yard at break, I coasted up to a senior slog as he practised netting a basketball and whispered, 'What's all this about Vinny nicking old Strang's keys?'

A few months ago he'd have told me to get lost, but my reputation had grown since blinding Vinny Litner and breaking Tony Trevino's slammer record, and he eyed me with a glint of respect.

'Where d'you hear that?'

'Chinese whispers.'

Whistling though his teeth, he swaggered away to spread the rumour.

The afternoon passed off as usual – four hours' wood-slashing in the rain under the weary, dripping gaze of good old Harry Headcase, followed by a *left-right, left-right, quick march!* back to supper. All the time I worked in the woods, the Predator's keys dangled before my eyes – I couldn't for the life of me remember whether or not I'd double-locked his secret door. If he realized it was me and put me back in the slammer, I'd go nuts. I was counting down the days to my escape, seven or eight – ten max.

All at once I was filled with a terrible dread.

The following morning, as drowsy slogs got stuck into slimy porridge, and as I was busy transferring my unswallowed Kalmasol pills to my trouser pocket for disposal later, the Predator strode in and bellowed, 'Freeze!'

All around me, spoons stopped halfway to mouths.

'Someone has removed a set of keys from my office. I'm willing to be lenient . . . I'm even prepared to overlook the matter – provided the individual concerned owns up immediately.'

Everyone sat stock-still. Dinner ladies stood by their trolleys.

'Don't be afraid, nothing will happen to you – you have my word.'

Mr Strang's word – imagine!

'Very well then, I'll offer a reward to any boy who raises a hand and says he knows where they are; twenty-five pounds, no questions asked.'

Nothing. 'Fifty pounds.'

Slogs exchanged glances, looked around for a hand to go up, and amazingly, one did. Archie!

The Predator's eyebrows lifted. 'Yes, young man – you have something to tell me?'

Archie made his way nervously forward and stretched to whisper in Mr Strang's ear. We probably expected a smile to light up the Predator's face. Instead, he rolled his eyes like Hardy does when Laurel comes out with something particularly stupid.

'No you can't be excused to *take a leak*,' he groaned to howls of laughter. 'Return to your place,' he snapped, then took out his mobile and made several calls issuing instructions for every dormitory to be thoroughly searched.

'Hands on heads, gentlemen, and God help anyone who moves a muscle.'

We sat there until our arms bled. I looked across at Skinny Hitler, who wore the lazy smirk of a spectator looking forward to a public flogging.

Footsteps – caretaker Yardley Giles waving a set of keys at his master as though bringing home the Holy Grail. Mr Strang tried not to show his relief as he listened to the hero's whispered report. Then he looked up and gazed at us all.

'Mr Litner, you surprise me.'

Skinny Hitler nearly fell off the planet. *Me?* he mouthed.

'Yes, sir – you, sir.' The Predator curled a finger.

Arms spread in innocence, Vinny Litner trailed out like a condemned man.

'Didn't think he had it in him, Marcus, did you?' Shelly murmured.

'No.'

Refusing to confess, Litner was flung in the slammer and handed a six-month extension to his sentence. The case against him was laughable, consisting merely of the missing item being found under his mattress. I was amazed that any young offender, however shady, could be so casually convicted. Imagine a judge pronouncing, *The body was found on the defendant's doorstep – the defendant's obviously the murderer!*

Lying awake that night, I pictured Vinny curled up shivering in the slammer. Days went by; I heard he was going round the twist. He had been a couple of months short of release, and now he was facing another six for something he hadn't done. I knew the feeling. He was taking the rap for me, like I once took the rap for him. Then we heard that Vinny was so low, old Doughnut had increased his meds to two pink pills – enough to tranquillize an elephant.

My revenge was complete – but it wasn't sweet.

Counting down the days. Head clear, fitness levels rising. I was like a greyhound straining in its box: patience, boy, calmly now, calmly.

One niggling worry was that one of my coopmates would betray my no-dope chewing-gum trick, since I was the only one still pulling it, but so far it remained safe. Meanwhile I kept taking every opportunity to pore over books and maps to pinpoint nearest towns, roads and railway lines, and to learn more about local terrain, rivers and lakes.

I had no specific plan – never did plan my escapes. I'd reach a moment of desperation, grab whatever dough I'd saved, spare kit and sleeping bag, and head for Victoria coach station. If I couldn't face the coach and had the cash, I jumped a train. When I was older, I bussed it to the outskirts, found the start of the motorway and stuck out my thumb. But this was different. I needed to be organized and focused. I needed to talk to Shannon, because I wasn't just doing a runner, I was planning to damage Dovedale. That was my only plan: head for Shannon's place – assuming she wrote back, assuming they'd read her my letter at Runningdene. If I hadn't heard from her by September 1st, I'd forget Shannon and go. Far away as possible in as little time as possible – and vanish.

Meantime, Vinny Litner had confessed to stealing the keys! He must have cracked. It's no good, I told myself. You've got to own up.

What? After what that scumbag did to you?

He's going crazy in there.

Good.

What if he tries to top himself?

They watch out for that – forget it.

I can't!

Why not, for crying out loud?

I can't have him beat my endurance record.

Confessing could jeopardize your escape.

Nothing is gonna jeopardize my escape.

It was time to do the decent thing. I went to the Predator's office straight after breakfast. No answer.

'What is it?'

He was coming down the corridor, puffy-eyed and blowing his hooter.

'We need to talk, sir.'

'I'm busy,' he said, unlocking the door, going in and throwing his briefcase on the desk.

'It's about your keys,' I said, following him in.

'What about my keys?'

'I know who took them.'

'Congratulations! Only I believe the culprit was apprehended some time ago. Good day!'

He hung up his raincoat, sat down at his desk.

'Vinny Litner never touched your keys, sir.'

He didn't have time for any of this. 'Get to class!' he said, and lifted the phone to make a call. Seeing I hadn't moved, he said, 'Have we overdone the medication, boy, or is surgery required?'

'You convicted the wrong slog.'

'He confessed!'

'He was desperate. He would have owned up to anything.'

A flicker of interest. 'Have you evidence of a wrongful conviction?'

I nodded.

'Quite the budding detective. Get out!' He laughed, and lifted the phone again.

'Vinny couldn't haven't done it, sir – because I did.'

He stopped dialling and replaced the phone. 'What did you say?'

'It was me.'

'It was you,' he echoed.

'Your office wasn't locked. I sat where you're sitting, tried the drawers.'

I had his full attention now.

'The cash didn't tempt me. The keys did.'

He was looking at me strangely. I could see the wheels spinning in his head. Without taking his eyes off me, he rose slowly and closed the door. Then he perched on the edge of the desk and folded his arms.

'What did you do with my keys?'

'Planted them under Vinny's mattress.'

'Before that?'

I stood there, hesitating, like a chess player before a risky move.

'I tried the keys out on your Strictly Private door.'

His face didn't change. He was trying to decide whether my move was brilliant or bluff. 'Really? Were you tempted to . . . ?'

'Yes.'

'Anything interesting or usual?'

'The whole thing was quite impressive.'

He sniffed and unfolded a fresh handkerchief to wipe his nose. 'What precisely impressed you?'

'How meticulously put together they all were . . . all the detail . . . and the way you lit them from below, like they were really flying and in danger . . .'

Colour drained from his face. I half wanted to re-assure him that it was no big deal. Why shouldn't a grown man have his little tucked-away hobby? But to him it was obviously sensitive and private.

'The sound-effects and searchlights working together were pretty cool.'

He gazed at me, hand massaging his throat, like a man anticipating the hangman's noose.

'That would explain why I found the door not properly locked.' His voice was croaky, a chess master ambushed by a novice.

'Don't worry about Email,' I said.

'What?'

'I've been telling him for years to get off his backside and join the air force.'

Folding his arms, he contemplated the floor. Sometimes, if you stare long enough at a chessboard, you suddenly see a way out.

He looked up brightly. 'So, you like my little project?'

'I do.'

'Glad to hear it, because you realize you were looking at a *research project* I was asked to undertake by a prestigious American university . . . new ways of engaging young offenders' imaginations and skills. The hypothesis I'm investigating is whether wayward youths might benefit from creative pastimes of this nature – you follow? With a military theme to engage their interests. So you see, Marcus, I'm *trying out* this idea, examining how it might look in practice. Interesting, don't you think?'

I nodded nervously. The grand master was digging deep.

'I can't imagine what you thought you'd stumbled on,' he chuckled, 'but I have to say' – suddenly serious – 'I'm shocked.'

Not content with wriggling out of mate, he wanted to turn the tables.

'Entering my office without permission, going through my desk, *sitting* at my desk! Taking my keys and trying them out – need I go on?'

I said nothing. Stroking his chin, he said, 'Some people might feel this merited a doubling of your sentence. What would you say to that?'

'Not a good move, sir.'

'I beg your pardon?'

'If I'm this bad after seven months in Dovedale, what's another seven gonna do?'

He smiled. It was all a game – slogs for pawns.

'Don't look so worried, I'm not a vindictive man and I suppose you should take credit for sheer bloody nerve, so' – fixing me with his most reasonable smile – 'I might be willing to overlook this transgression . . . provided you're willing to keep my project under your hat . . . until I'm ready to formally introduce it?'

I nodded carefully.

'So, Marcus, we have a deal?'

I hesitated. Careful now.

'You get to keep your secret, sir . . . what's my cut?'

'I told you, I let you off.'

'With respect, sir, it's not enough.'

We stared at each other, unblinking.

'Take a seat.'

I sat down.

'What do you want?'

'My freedom?' I smiled.

'Ah' – he laughed – 'that's one thing I have limited control over. And how would I justify your release to Miss Rice-Bird, not to mention society? However' – plucking ideas from the air – 'I could arrange for you to have your visits reinstated.'

'I'd appreciate that, but only if you included my coopmates, who actually performed wonders in Runningdene.'

'That's debatable, and in any case, I couldn't possibly get such a proposal past Miss Rice-Bird.'

'Then how about easing up on us, all those cold baths and dawn runs?'

'Hmm,' he went and gazed at the ceiling. Observing him, I realized that even though my heart was going like a piston, I wasn't afraid of him any more. I was afraid of what he could *do*, but not of him.

He sat up, met my gaze. 'How do I know you'll keep your side of the bargain, Marcus?'

'How do I know you'll keep yours, sir?'

Checkmate.

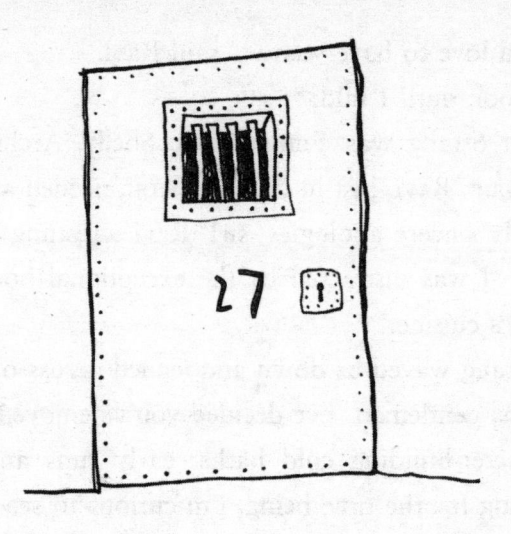

I'd gone the distance with the Beast of Dovedale, I'd won concessions for my mates and I should have been feeling good, but I wasn't. I was anxious – and couldn't concentrate in class. My escape bid was getting closer and I was afraid that the Predator might have something up his sleeve. Man, I was jumpy.

'What's the matter, boy?' said Mr Kyte. 'Isn't your medication working?'

All morning I was tense and drained. But I needn't have worried. Halfway through lunch Mr Strang appeared, trailing a boy behind him. Slogs on every table nudged each other as Skinny Hitler, wearing a sorry sneer, returned to his place after 107 hours in the slammer.

'Your record's safe, Marcus!' Shelly congratulated me across the table.

'Litner must've grovelled,' said Archie.

'I'd love to have seen it,' said Ravi.

'Look out!' I said.

Mr Strang was coming over. Shelly, Archie and I stood up. Ravi, lost in cheesy ravioli, needed an elbow.

'My sincere apologies, sir!' Ravi wrestling with his chair. 'I was distracted by the exceptional bouquet of today's cuisine.'

Strang waved us down and leaned across our table. 'News, gentleman. I've decided you've enjoyed enough character-building cold baths, early runs and wood clearing for the time being. I'm curious to see whether my generosity is rewarded by an all-round improvement in behaviour.'

Reserving a hard warning glance for me, he turned on his heels and left the dining hall. Stunned and delighted, my coopmates clapped each other on the back.

'Still against co-operation?' said Shelly, shooting me a look.

'*Toe the line for times sublime!*' Ravi sang.

'How could I have got it so wrong?' I said, joining in the bull.

'And the first thing I'm going to do,' said Ravi, throwing a meaty arm around my shoulders, 'is turn my chest of drawers into an altar to saintly Mr Strang, and give thanks to him every night.'

'You'll have to forgive me, Rav, if I don't join you.'

'You're too cynical,' Shelly told me. 'What could Strang possibly get out of it?'

'Post!' someone cried, and I watched while a slog went round distributing a armful of letters and parcels. Just as I'd been doing for days, I waited for him to read an envelope and look up and find me. But our only mail was a card and parcel for Shelly – inspected by old Moses as he opened it. My heart sank, the same thought tormenting me: Fiona had opened my letter and decided it wouldn't do for Shannon to be corresponding with the deviant who led her into the sea.

Then I felt a hand on my shoulder, Moses slipping me a letter and moving on. I looked at the envelope – pale green with pink trimming. Crooked handwriting. *Care of Mr C. Trust.*

'Who's it from?' they all wanted to know.

'The Queen. Pestering me again about that knighthood.'

At break time I sat on a wall and opened the typed and printed-out letter.

```
                              17 Nuthatch Crescent
                                        Glenview
                                       Salthaven


                                      August 26


Dear Marcus,
   It was brilliant meeting you too.
I felt like I'd always known you.
```

Fiona didn't want to read me your letter, but agreed in the end I had a right.

There's so much I don't know about you, like what books you read, what's your star sign — I'm Taurus — and what planet you're from! More important, I'm a bit worried about your plans. I'd really like to help if I can.

Give me a call sometime!

Love, Shannon

In a PS she inserted her phone number.

I folded the letter in my pocket, vowing to memorize everything before destroying it. I wanted to call Shannon right away, but Dovedale's pay phones were situated right outside Mrs Armitage's office, and she had ears like a bat.

I stretched out on the wall, gazed at the sky and made my decision. Today was Wednesday. Tomorrow I'd attempt a brief dry run. Friday night – I'm out of here.

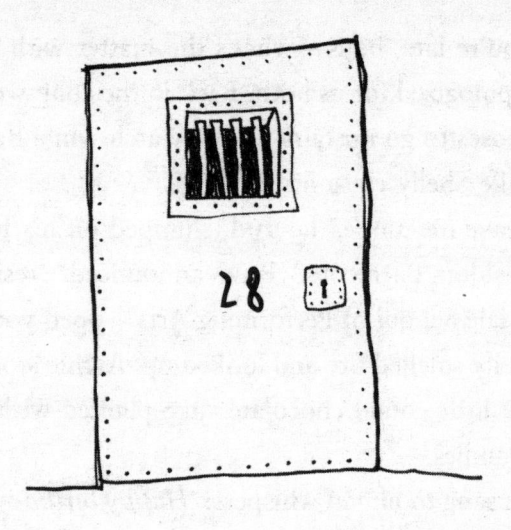

Shelly read his birthday card and tore it in two. He was depressed and wanted to be left alone. The card, which I picked up off the floor, had TO OUR DARLING SON on the front, a boy swinging a golf club and 16 emblazoned on a trophy. Inside was written: *I hope you have a nice birthday, but I was very disappointed with your whole attitude in our last phone call. With rather less affection than usual – Yours, Mum.*

Shelly got more depressed as the day went on and ended up in a cubicle in the jacks, refusing to budge.

'C'mon,' I whispered. 'We got a surprise for you.'

The bathroom was deserted, everyone in bed.

'Shell, I'm not moving till you come out.'

After ten minutes of me sitting on the floor, whistling, he emerged white as a sheet and off we went – straight into Clarence Trust.

'You're late, boys – what's the matter with you?'

I apologized for us both. Back in the coop we waited for Moses to go upstairs. I kept watch while Ravi tried to make Shelly close his eyes.

'Leave me alone,' he said, slumped on his bed.

'Sheldon Barnicote,' Ravi announced, 'residing at Dovedale School of Performing Arts – open your eyes!'

Shelly smelled fire and looked up. Archie stood there with a little round chocolate cake planted with sixteen tiny candles.

We sang to him in whispers: *'Happy birthday to you, happy birthday to you, happy birthday, dear Shelly, happy birthday to you.'*

Shelly sat up, flames in his eyes.

'Blow them out, and make a wish!' I said.

Shelly gazed at his cake.

'Before someone comes, man!' said Ravi.

'In a minute,' Shelly said, eyes watering.

'Before I drool to death . . .' Ravi was saying when we became aware of Moses standing in the doorway, stopped in his tracks by the sight of a slog sitting on his bed with a lighted cake in his lap. Having food of any kind in your coop was punishable by death.

'It won't happen again,' murmured Ravi, 'for at least another twelve months.'

Moses stood transfixed.

Shelly looked up. 'Fancy a slice, Mr Trust?'

'I might just take you up on that.'

'Coming up!' said Shelly. 'Only how the hell do we cut it?'

Archie produced a smuggled plastic kitchen knife. Shelly blew out his candles and meditated a moment. I offered Moses a chair – he politely declined. We stood around munching cake in companionable silence.

'Many happy returns, son,' mumbled Moses, turning to go.

'You OK, Mr Trust?' I said. 'You seem kind of distracted.'

'The scales are falling from my eyes, Mr King.'

He went out – we all looked at each other.

'What the blazes did he mean by that?' said Ravi.

I went after him. 'Mr Trust – what's going on?'

He turned. 'What's it to you, Mr King?'

'I'm here to learn, aren't I?'

'There's nothing here.'

'Then maybe you can teach me something.'

He laid a hand on my shoulder and smiled. 'You're looking at a blind man . . . one who is only just learning to see again. A thousand books I've read, without getting any nearer the truth . . . and if I seem a little disorientated, it's because the dark is so much easier to endure than the light.'

With that, he turned to go upstairs.

'Mr Trust?'

He stopped halfway up.

'In case I don't get a chance . . . thanks for everything.'

Back in the coop, Shelly was opening his present, a little something wrapped in foil with a bunch of daisies attached, and a handmade card, which read:

> To *la belle Shell* – *have a nice one!*
> *Love from all your mates*
> *(except Archie, who prefers 'best wishes')*

Shelly looked at the clumsy package in his hands.

'Open it!' said Archie, madly clicking his fingers.

Shelly unpicked the foil – gazed at someone's make-up case, neat, slim and expensive. Unzipped it and peeked inside – took out eye shadow, lipstick, compact case – the works. Amazed – 'Where did you get this?'

Ravi and I shrugged, like – *Don't look at us!* Shelly looked at Archie.

'All in a day's work, mate.'

'Who's it belong to?'

'You.'

'Who did it belong to?'

'I enjoy library periods' – Archie whistled innocently – 'don't you, Shell?'

'Mrs Armitage.' Shelly laughed. 'There's going to be trouble.'

'Enjoy it while you can,' said Archie.

Around midnight, I sat up and whispered, 'Shelly, you awake?'

'Yes.'

'Got a minute?'

I invited him to join me at the window. He was wearing nothing but a bath-towel evening gown. His face was transformed by eye shadow, mascara and lipstick and he reeked of jasmine, so I had to keep reminding myself I was talking to a bloke.

'Fancy some action, Shell?' I whispered.

He looked at me warily.

'Relax, I'm not planning a revolution.'

'What are you planning?'

I looked past him to make sure the others were asleep. 'I'm getting out,' I whispered.

He frowned at me. *Are you cracked, or what?*

'Listen, Shell, I've been a model slog, done everything they asked, even took my meds, but this place is like Snakes and Ladders. Just when you make it to the top, you find yourself back at the bottom! I've had it, man. This hotel's too tense, I'm checking out.'

Shelly gazed at me. 'Why you telling me this?'

'I want to invite you along. Even Kalmasoled you'd make it. I'm planning a short rehearsal tomorrow night, the real thing Friday. I'm counting on a fullish moon to see by. First stop Salthaven, look in on Shannon and check out her ideas for shining a light on this hole.'

'What do you mean?'

'The UN article backed up by our first-hand accounts

of all the abuse. Get on the radio, hook up with some reporters – or something.'

He nodded. Kind of liked the idea.

'From there, I'm not sure. If the press won't bite, and we're still free, a bus to Three Bridges, train to London, hop on a ferry and check out friends I got in *la belle France*. Head south to the sun. I can just see us, Shell – instead of Christmas in Dovedale, flicking a Frisbee on a beach in Morocco!'

I saw the fear and excitement in his eyes.

'Salthaven is only forty-five miles, Shell. Nothing much between there and here but woods and wilderness, the odd river, lake and farm, so we'd carry what grub and water we can.'

Shelly gazed at me – scorn and admiration.

'I think we'd make a good team, Shell, I really do.'

'I *knew* you were up to something.'

'It'd be less lonely and more fun.'

'You told anyone?'

'I thought about letting the others in, but—'

'Archie and Ravi? You're joking.'

'Well, what do you say?'

We were looking out at a star-lit sky – miles and miles of trees and hills – dark, lonely and enticing.

'Listen, Marcus, I want out as much as you,' he whispered, 'but I want out for good. I've no ambition to be the new Tony Trevino. I don't want to get caught in the wilds somewhere and dragged back here in disgrace to be told I've got another six months to do. Way too risky.'

'Life's about risks, man! Those who dare and those who duck.'

'Shhh!'

Ravi groaned in his sleep, looking for his mum.

'Some risks are worth taking, Marcus, some aren't. I told you, doesn't matter how much I hate it, I'm going to keep toeing the line if it means getting out for sure.'

'And I told you – toeing the line becomes a habit.'

'Don't worry about me, Marcus, it's under control,' said Shelly, rubbing heat into his bare shoulders. 'This is the last time I dress up in Dovedale. From now on I do exactly what I'm told without a word. And when I get out, I'll carry on playing the game – I'll play football and wear boring clothes and go round grunting like real boys are supposed to. I'll bide my time, and when I'm seventeen my parents won't see me for dust. I'll work and get my own flat and dress how I want, and be who I want and no one will be able to stop me. Until then, I'm a good boy – you understand, Marcus?' he said, jabbing me in the chest with a finger. 'I'm sick of being yelled at here and at home. I'm sick of the indignity and abuse – I can't stand it any more. Nobody' – seizing me by the collar, eyes blazing – 'is going to dictate to me ever again – you hear me? I've had it up to *here*, Marcus,' he sobbed, dropping his head onto my shoulder. 'I can't take it any more. My way of getting *out* is staying *put* – you understand?'

'It's cool, Shell, it's cool . . .' I said, patting him tenderly.

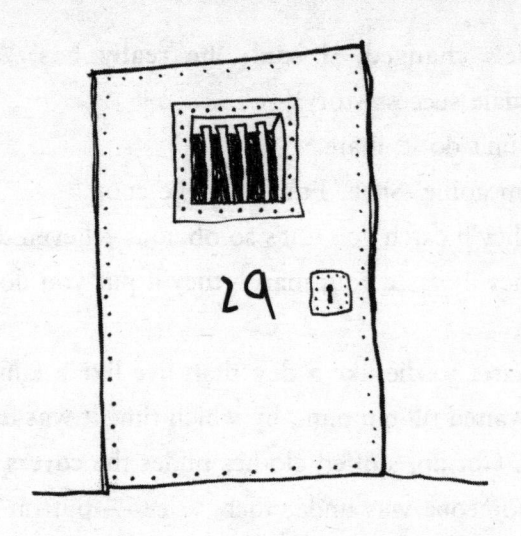

Thursday, dry-run day. Nothing must go wrong – no trouble of any kind. At morning registration I answered my name crisply, and kept my head so far down during lessons, Mr Kyte was heard to announce, 'Mr King, I do believe we're making some progress.'

'Thank you, sir.'

Shelly collared me in the showers after gym, eyes filled with confusion.

'I can't decide,' he whispered, 'whether I envy you or think you're a fool, but listen, Marcus – don't do it, it's crazy.'

'You know, Shell, I could imagine us being friends on the outside.'

'Don't change the subject.'

'And Ravi. Maybe even Archie?'

Shelly twisted up his face, like, *I don't think so.*

'He's changed,' I said, 'he really has. Another Dovedale success story!'

'Don't do it, mate.'

'I'm going, Shell. I'm flying the coop.'

'They'll catch you – it's so obvious – I even dreamed it! They'll waste you, man – they'll put you down like a dog!'

'Better to die like a dog than live like a lamb.'

I waited till ten p.m., by which time it was dark and quiet. Got up, stuffed clothes under the covers to look like someone was under there asleep – put on trainers and regulation rain jacket over my pyjamas and made my way down through the snoring building towards the entrance hall.

The night duty whip and security guard used the secretary's office as their base. I could smell cigarette smoke and hear a radio. I passed five fire-escape doors going down, all alarmed. Ground-floor exit doors and windows were also alarmed, all except the front door. A strategically mounted mirror allowed anyone in the office to have a fairly good view of the front door and the area around it. The mirror was my biggest problem, though thanks to the Iceberg's obsession with economy, the entrance hall was poorly lit.

I waited in the shadows. Another few steps and I was looking into the office via the distant mirror, watching Moses, standing with his back turned, and beyond him the security guard, all in black and seated, chatting together. I darted over to the door, pressed myself flat against the wall. Never taking my eye off the mirror, I lifted the gigantic key out of its box, inserted it in the door and gingerly opened it, removing the key. The Iceberg had an aversion to squeaking doors, and the caretaker regularly oiled the front door's ancient hinges, making them silent. One last glance in the mirror . . .

Locking the door carefully from the outside, I went quietly down the steps and crossed the forecourt and the deserted car park, skirted the spooky ornamental fountain, climbed the stile and headed down the track into Strapps Wood. It was raining – no sign of the moon.

I set off along the route I'd taken on that last fateful Hare and Hounds, until the rain got through to my pyjamas and I turned back, feeling my way in the pitch dark. Trees swayed and creaked in the wind. Rain rattled the treetops and spattered the leaves. The darkness was awesome, a taste of what faced me tomorrow night. It was a darkness that didn't begin or end, one that triggered all your senses, one I must learn quickly to embrace instead of fear. Trotting back, the only resistance to the dark came from the secretary's window, and the sickly glow of nightlights in deserted corridors. I crept up to a window, peered in and saw, across the hall, Moses and the security guard sitting reading newspapers.

Approaching the front door, I carefully unlocked it, and squeezed inside. Glued to the mirror, I removed my muddy shoes, locked the door and replaced the key. Still watching the mirror, and trying not to drip on the floor, I started for the stairs – and stopped at the sound of a newspaper slapped down, the scrape of a chair, the sight of a shadow flung into the corridor. No choice but grab the nearest hiding spot – a shadowy gap behind a boxed fire extinguisher – and prepare to fake an episode of sleepwalking.

Moses went straight past me and up the stairs.

I followed at a safe distance and, while he carried on up to check the senior coops, spirited myself back to bed.

I woke before the alarm and lay listening to the dawn chorus, heart beating fast.

My last Dovedale morning.

I pulled my no-dope dodge one last time without a wobble. My head was clear, my veins fast-flowing rivers! I was ready. I observed my coopmates over breakfast, how young and vulnerable they looked. I looked around at all the other slogs tucking blindly into their cereals, heads in the trough, deaf to the sound of sharpening knives.

I made my bed and tidied my area for the last time. In class I played the docile student. Mr Kyte rocked back and forth on his heels, a look of satisfaction on his face.

I caught Shelly glancing over at me and smiled. He looked away.

The afternoon dragged. As Harry Headcase led every Dovedale slog round the field, humping backpacks stuffed with stones, I counted down the hours and did my best to look lively.

'You're not even trying, lad,' he groaned.

I was conserving fuel for the long night ahead, and could think of nothing else – until a junior slog barged into the changing rooms afterwards and said, 'Oi, Noodle Head, the Iceberg wants ya.'

The others looked at me.

'Relax, bros! She wants to make me Head Boy. I might just take her up on it.'

I tidied myself up, calmed myself down. It was a slow hike to the office, brain shooting off at angles. When I knocked on her door and went in, I saw the Predator was there as well, saw the look on both their faces.

'Stand up straight,' said the Iceberg.

I was standing up straight.

'Who's been spreading malicious rumours?'

I looked from the Iceberg to Mr Strang, who was staring at me, arms folded.

'Lost your tongue, Mr King?' said the Iceberg. 'It's been running pretty freely lately, hasn't it?'

'I'd like to help, miss, I really would, but—'

'You've been spreading stories about Mr Strang's private quarters.'

'I don't think so.'

'Honesty, Mr King, is always the best policy.'

'I told no one, not a living soul. I'm a keep-my-word sort of bloke.'

'Let's take a walk, shall we?' said the Iceberg.

Turned out to be a short stroll out of her office and into his – Mr Strang unlocking it and standing aside to let us in.

'So, young man, what do you suppose lies behind that door?' demanded the Iceberg, pointing a painted fingernail.

I looked urgently at Mr Strang – but he wasn't returning my calls.

'Mr Strang is working on a research project,' I said, 'sponsored by an American university.'

'Really?'

'Model aircraft . . . a new beginning for idle misfits.'

The Iceberg and the Predator exchanged glances. Then he took out a familiar bunch of keys, unlocked the door and invited me to enter.

I went in and stood there. My mind's eye saw swooping planes and searchlights, but all that was gone – the air was empty. The workshop trestle table, once home to glues, paints and Stanley knives, was now packed with classroom textbooks and dictionaries, boxes of pens, whiteboard markers. The armchair where Mr Strang once relaxed with a cigar and a nip of whisky was replaced by an exercise bike and a pair of weights for toning up muscles. Permanently drawn curtains were thrown open to the light. A window was open, ruffling the curtains.

'If you must know Mr Strang's dark secret,' said the Iceberg, 'he regularly uses the exercise bike and weights to maintain his fitness. Perhaps you'd like to spread that rumour instead.'

So complete was the transformation from playroom to stockroom that, for a fleeting moment, my brain whirled backwards like a clock gone mad, and I thought, *I'm going nuts*. I started searching for evidence overlooked on the floor – a piece of undercarriage, a propeller, a heat-seeking missile – nothing.

'What have you to say for yourself now, young man?'

I wanted to tell her that her deputy was a liar and a coward – the worst kind of middle-aged offender – but opted for silence.

She stared at me. 'You may have nothing to say, but I have plenty. You are a sick, delinquent child, one of the worst I've had the misfortune to work with . . . clearly determined to wreck all my efforts to reform you. I shall be speaking to Dr Cavendish about your medication, because it obviously hasn't been strong enough. In the meantime, I'm handing him over to you, Mr Strang.'

'I'll put him in solitary, until the doctor can see him.'

'Whatever you decide, Mr Strang – just take him away.'

There goes the weekend! I thought, as the Iceberg

swept out and Mr Strang locked his *stockroom* and his office, and motioned me to follow.

I walked beside him, barely keeping up. 'I kept my side of the deal, Mr Strang.'

This had no effect.

'I understand why you're doing this, but your secret was safe.'

This only made him walk faster.

'Why the over-reaction?' Nearly running now. 'You could have made it into a real project, slogs making model planes. I'd have been the first to sign up!'

When we reached the stairs descending to the slammer, I stopped and said, 'No, sir, please.'

'I'm waiting,' he said, holding the door.

'I'm cooked enough as it is, don't you think?'

'Obviously not cooked enough.'

'I'm not going down.'

'You want me to call security?'

'Put me down there and I might not be so keen to keep your secret.'

'Are you threatening me, boy?'

'Put me down there, and I'm never coming out.'

He raised a hand to hit me . . .

'Whoa! Easy, sir – you'll do yourself an injury.'

He glared at me – I moved closer. Softly now, eyeball to eyeball –

'You know my trouble, sir? I trust too easy, a chronic case of Compulsive Trust Disorder. You know your trouble, Mr Strang? You don't trust anyone or anything. No wonder you're such a warped individual.'

He looked at me as if I'd just pulled a sharpened stake from behind my back and driven it into his chest. Then, standing up straight, he found a peculiar smile and murmured, 'Get to your lessons, boy.'

We stood a minute gazing at each other.

'Thank you, sir.'

Then he turned on his heels and walked away.

'Yo! Boss,' I called, 'take care of old Email.'

'All your property will be returned when you leave.'

At homework time in the den, making sure Archie and Ravi didn't notice, I emptied my school bag – a handy lightweight little number that strapped onto my back – and repacked it with biscuits, bread filched from the dining hall, fruit, two plastic 500 ml bottles of water and all the dough I had in the world – a fiver and a pocketful of change, plus the tenner Shelly had silently slipped me at supper – leaving just enough space to squeeze in clean underwear and spare tracksuit.

Getting ready for bed, I looked out for the last time at the sunset burning through the woods. Darkness was falling fast – my heart was running away with itself. I always felt a build-up of tension before any escape, but this wasn't St Vincent's Primary School or Brockwell High and I felt sick with nerves.

I lay in bed, hands behind my head. The clock above

the door glowed faintly under the nightlight. I lay there, wondering how soon it would be before they discovered me missing – what form the search would take, how quickly they'd put an alert out on the railways.

Whips did night shifts one week in four, and Moses was on that final night. He was always particular about checking coops every twenty minutes, even if he only fired his torch into the room. But if you stayed awake, you noticed that like all the others he got sloppier as the night went on, and by ten he was only looking in twice an hour, by midnight once. The later I left it the better. On the other hand, I was afraid to lose escape time – wanted to be as far away as possible by dawn. I decided to wait until ten o'clock.

I closed my eyes and breathed. Every nerve-ending in my body was buzzing.

The moon sent a feeler in the window.

C'mon, Marcus, it's time.

All right – all right! Don't hassle me.

Lying there, heart beating – *This is it, this is* it.

Wait a sec. Floorboards creaking, old Moses on his rounds again.

I scrunched myself up small as I could. Heard him pause in the doorway, saw the beam of his torch flit round the coop and return to my bed. I heard him enter and come over to me. Heard him breathing, felt him lift the edge of the covers to make sure there was somebody under there.

Waited for him to check the coops on the floor above; waited for him to go all the way downstairs again. And then it went quiet – my heart hammering in the stillness. Damn! I thought. I never planned for this, never imagined I'd feel like turning over and going to sleep. My head was full of voices: *This is too big, too scary, too irrational . . . Don't feel bad about it . . . See out your sentence . . . It'll be all right this time.*

Then I thought about Strang cracking the whip for the next twelve months, and Dr Doughnut jacking up the dope, and not seeing Shannon again, and the brutal injustice of it hit me like a bucket of ice, and I was up and out of bed.

You can't fight these people – they hold all the cards.
We'll see about that.

Shaking myself down and shivering, I put on tracksuit, jumper, trainers and rain jacket. Ravi slept like the dead and, prizing his pillow from under him, I dressed it in my pyjama top. I grabbed all the clothes left in my drawers and arranged everything under the covers to look like M. King – number 307 – was still there. Then I removed my homemade bookmark containing the UN article from my Bible and zipped it into a top pocket. Finally I left a packet of chocolate biscuits on the end of each of my coopmates' beds and, strapping my bag on my back, took a last look around. A feeling of calm came over me. Whatever happened tonight, however far I got or didn't get, I was doing what I said I'd do, choosing action over surrender. This was my body, my brain – it didn't belong to Dovedale.

This is *my* life and I want it *back*.

As I moved towards the door, I saw Shelly lying there watching me.

'Tell them I said something about a godparent in Scotland,' I whispered. 'Throw them off track.'

He nodded.

'See you, Shell – take care.'

I was almost out the door when he called out softly, 'Marcus?'

'What?'

'Good luck.'

Eyes stinging, I started down the stairs, down through the familiar building, taking the final flight one creaking step at a time, pausing as I reached the dim, wide entrance hall. Silence – just the pumping of my heart. Then voices from the secretary's office. Holding my breath in the shadows at the foot of the stairs, I crept forward until I could see them in the mirror – the security guard rolling a cigarette, and Clarence Trust perched on the rim of the desk, lost in thought. Measuring the distance across the hall and keeping an eye on the mirror, I made my move to the front door and stretched for the key.

A burst of chatter from the office checked me – I flattened myself against the wall and stood, key in hand, watching, listening. The office went quiet – just the radio. Leaning out from the wall, I could see the security guard smoking and reading – old Moses opening a window. Unlocking the front door, I replaced the key in its box and, still watching the mirror, opened the door without a sound, just enough let myself out, shutting it softly behind me. Heart beating wildly, I started down the steps.

The night was mine! *This is it, I'm out of here* – or so I thought.

Someone was standing there, a stone's throw away. For a moment I thought it was a statue I hadn't noticed before, but the statue was lifting a burning speck of light to its lips, a thin cigar. He was looking straight at me. He'd been tipped off and was waiting. Shelly, you lousy . . .

Wait a second, he had no eyes – he had his back to me, he was looking the other way. He was standing there, contemplating the sky, puffing on his cigar. I melted backwards into ivy under the porch. As I watched, the Predator dropped his cigar, crushed it underfoot and walked away, getting smaller along the lane in the direction of his cottage.

I was out in the open and running – across the forecourt and staff car park and past the eerie ornamental fountain, and with the moon showing the way, vaulted the stile and sprinted down the track into Strapps Wood. Moments later the moon disappeared, throwing the wood into darkness.

I stopped for breath – looked back. Through the trees I could just make out the roofs and chimneys of Dovedale against the night sky. I thought of Ravi and Archie finding me gone in the morning, imagined them feeling more vulnerable than ever, and tried to shake off the thought.

I jogged on, getting used to the dark, deeper into the woods. Even with the moon hidden, there was light floating like vapour and I tried following the route I'd taken on that last Hare and Hounds, tried to spot the clearing where I went to Ravi's defence, but things look different at night, and soon I didn't know where I was and didn't recognize anything. Every time the treetops parted, I paused to track the North Star and pointed myself north and east.

My energy amazed me. Afraid to stop, I kept walking, jogging, walking and jogging, keeping a steady pace. Tracks weaved this way and that, taking me out of my way and back again. Sometimes two or three tracks tried to confuse me, but I seized one or the other without stopping, like a mariner in a gale clinging to the stars. After what seemed like hours I emerged in the open and could make out the distant outline of Fox Rock – and imagined I saw Shelly way ahead, running like the wind.

Now for a switch of direction. Instead of chalking my initials on Fox Rock and curving back round towards Dovedale, I veered east towards a broad belt of forest called Croxley Wood, which I'd studied in the library. On the far side of the forest, I hoped to cross a broad valley between hills and keep weaving between isolated farms until I reached Salthaven. The night was cold, but I was burning up and stripped off my jacket and jumper, tying them round my waist as I ran.

Once inside Croxley Wood, I relied on the moon. When it slid into cloud, I had to slow right down or stop altogether, groping forward in the dark. Even with the moon blazing, I found myself bamboozled time and again by jungles of spiky brambles, losing time hacking my way through. Sometimes tracks ran clear, sometimes I couldn't tell if I was on a path or not, or it slipped into a boggy depression and I had to wait for the moon to pull me out the other side. It had all looked so simple in the library.

Suddenly I was tired. Confident that even if caught in the next two minutes I'd gone ten miles further than Tony Trevino, I dropped to the ground, un-slung my bag and took a few mouthfuls of water. Then I capped the bottle again and re-packed it.

The silence – disturbed only by the rustling of leaves – was awesome. Looking around at the endless trees leaning and stretching skyward, I felt small and scared and a little voice whispered, *You can always turn back*. I smiled at the thought of lobbing a pebble at my old window, praying one of my coopmates would wake and smuggle me back in.

No, Marcus, there's no going back.

I zipped up my bag and ran on, seeking out clearings in the wood to read the sky. And then the trees petered out and the landscape rose like a tidal wave in the dark, and I was climbing a narrow track through prickly gorse under a watchful moon. Good, this is good. I should get a view from up here and find a lake to my left. The path climbed randomly, twisting this way and that. When I thought I'd reached the top, there was more to climb. The maps I'd studied were too stingy to include the contours of high ground; you picked up clues best you could. The hill evened out, and still it climbed, leading me on over stony ground until finally I was on top of the world, and there – look, bright as a mirror! – a lake. Except it was off to my right when it should have been over to my left. My star-reading was a few million miles out.

The climb had finished me off. I sank to my knees, feet and legs on fire. I'd just run and walked further than ever in my whole life. The lake before me was around fifteen miles from Dovedale. When planning this, I had visions of them letting a couple of Alsatians sniff my pyjamas before unleashing them, like they did to track Trevino, and I'd determined to push hard through the night, taking short breaks and putting twenty miles behind me before dawn. Five to go and an hour's darkness left. I ran on.

The night was losing its intensity; the first pale wash

of dawn threatened in the east. I wanted to keep going but couldn't stop myself sinking to the ground. Gulping water, I saved some for morning. I thought about food, but was too whacked. With my bag for a pillow, I lay down beneath the vast star-sprinkled sky. I thought I'd sleep right away, but my mind was racing and the moon was too bright.

Somebody switch that light out!

The moon vanished, drizzle began falling out of a starless sky and I put my jumper and thin jacket back on, rubbed my arms and legs and snuggled up to a rock.

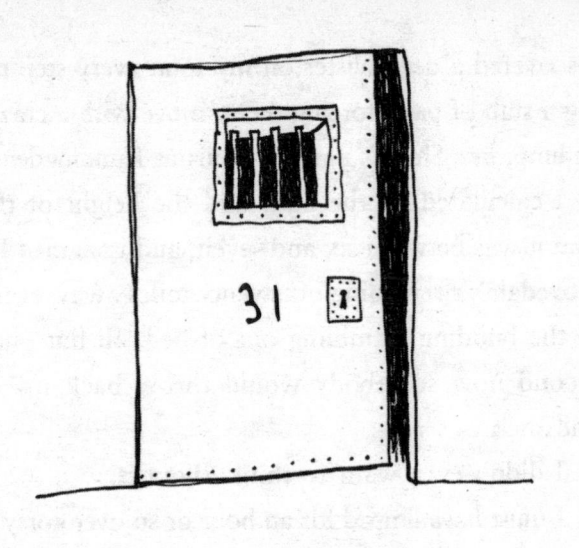

Next thing I knew it was light, and I found myself on a rocky hillside drenched in mist. I rubbed my eyes and searched the landscape for cops sweeping the ground with dogs – but all was still. Mist covered rocky slopes for miles around, and hung in shrubs and trees like washing, and suddenly I thought about my parents and sister. Had they been informed? I had to call them.

The world didn't look quite as scary now, though there wasn't a house in sight, no humans – no mammals at all, only birds singing unseen, or flitting bush to bush. Early bees droned in sparkling heather.

I got up and stretched. No sixty-second stampede to the bathroom. No bathroom. My body was stiff as wood. Munching a banana and beating myself up to get the blood going, I picked up my bag and started off again, legs buckling as I stumbled down the slope and discovered a deep blister on my foot, every step triggering a stab of pain, forcing me to move with a crazy kind of limp, like Shelly's partner Louis at Runningdene.

I calculated by the light and the height of the sun that it was between six and seven, and imagined I heard Dovedale's siren going off twenty miles away, every slog in the building stumbling out of bed, all but one. Any second now somebody would throw back my covers and then . . . ?

I didn't even want to think about it.

I must have limped for an hour or so over gorsy moorland before I hit the first serious setback – a river crossing my path. What had been a harmless thread on a map turned out wide as a motorway and almost as fast. Terrific. The good news – I'm probably heading in the right direction; the bad news – nowhere in sight to cross. On one map there may have been a dotted line crossing the river, a ford or bridge or something – geography was never my best subject. Living in South London, it didn't seem crucial. Little did I know. I stood on a flat rock and shielded my eyes. Swimming wasn't my best event either. I limped along the riverbank to find the narrowest point, but whichever way the river surged and weaved, it remained wide and fast and deep – and as if that wasn't bad enough, a distant sound stopped me in my tracks, made me instinctively cast about for cover. Looking back the way I'd come, I could hear – but couldn't see – a helicopter.

Right, that's it! I thought. Time to do a Ravi Sharma

– and I tore off all my clothes, stuffed them in my bag, slung it over my shoulder and slid into the river. A moment's grace, then – *bloody hell!* – the freezing current plucked me from the bank and dragged me downstream. Rolling into a clumsy one-armed side stroke, I held my bag out of the water and swam frantically. The river was like a creature I'd accidentally disturbed, grabbing me and trying to pull me under, and as I thrashed about, the bag slipped my grip and got snapped up and pitched downstream, round a bend and out of sight. My clothes, dough – everything!

With two free arms I struck out for the far shore until, tiring of the game, the river nudged me out of the rush and into shallows. Grappling with waist-high reeds, I crawled out of the swamp like the first human and collapsed, spewing water and shivering. I lay there, tickled by grass and insects, the sun on my back. No clothes, not even underpants. I could hear the laughter ringing out around Dovedale. Pictured Shannon's mum answering her front door.

I got up – no sight or sound of that helicopter – and tripped along the riverbank like Adam looking for Eve, praying my bag hadn't travelled too far or sunk without trace; praying if I moved fast enough I might spot it bobbing about on the— Look! What's that? A little way ahead, my side of the river, a family of water birds disturbed by something washed up under their nest among trailing branches.

'Relax, guys, me friendly . . .' I told the ducks, wading in to rescue my bag and fling it high onto the bank. Everything I owned was sodden, including the money and bookmark. I picked it open and found the UN article still intact – damp but legible. The morning air was cold on my skin. Spreading clothes and paper money over bushes to catch the sun, I hopped around naked, slapping myself to get the blood pumping. The sun was dissolving the mist and I guessed it was after eight or nine o'clock and old Kyte would be calling a three-man register, saying, 'Where's Mr King?' Word of my escape would have sparked a tongue-wagging frenzy at breakfast. What would Strangeboy and Skinny Hitler make of it? What would the Iceberg and the Predator be saying to each other? I really didn't care.

Then my ears pricked up. Damn! That helicopter again. I searched the distant sky, but couldn't see it. Tossed the ruined bread to the ducks, dragged on my saturated underwear and tracksuit, socks and shoes and started the long climb out of the valley. Reaching high ground, I looked back and there, loose in distant cloud like a flea on a cat, the helicopter.

Fear cut the legs from under me. I crouched down – riding the panic.

You can't fight these people, they hold all the cards. Oh yeah?

I drank the last of my water, holding onto the empty bottles in the hope of finding fresh. Then, navigating by the sun, I climbed on out of the valley, and the land-scape began to change. Sheep materialized – millions of them flung all over slopes and rocks – and soon I was clambering over ruined drystone walls. I kept going, squelching through mud, onward and upward. Now and then I stopped to recover my strength and search the sky behind me. Sometimes I spotted the chopper, sometimes I could only hear it, and my heart hammered – it was definitely looking for me. And yet it seemed to be restricting its search to a limit of about half a dozen miles, as though reluctant to believe a Kalmasoled slog could have got any further.

I pictured Shelly, Ravi and Archie trying to concentrate in class, keeping their fingers crossed for me – or secretly praying I'd get caught and come home to them – everyone wondering how far I'd get, whips and slogs discussing my chances. Then I saw myself bedraggled and shivering, delivered to Dovedale in handcuffs – pictured the Iceberg and Mr Strang swapping smiles, and a surge of energy swept me on.

I stumbled on an abandoned cottage, open to the sky, and sat down in the shade of its gaping entrance. I was getting desperately thirsty, but tried not to think about it. The sun was high, the heat fierce. After a time I didn't hear the chopper any more. I got up and pressed on.

I saw a house in the distance and aimed for it. It'd be risky meeting someone now, but apart from needing water I wanted to know where I was and how much further I had to go. And I wanted to call home and tell them I was OK, and phone Shannon to tell her I was coming.

As I climbed the rocky slope, I saw the house wasn't a house, but an old wooden hut. I climbed faster, ducking into the open door. The hut was dark and deserted. I made out a bench and a sheepskin rug, a row of bottles on the floor – all cruelly empty. Wait a minute – what's that? Above the bench a shelf, and on the shelf an unlabelled bottle on its own, this one full. Seizing it, I twisted out the cork and took a sniff. It smelled clean, sharp and fruity. I took a swig and went, *What the hell . . . ?* Every reasoning cell in my brain said *No!* Every other cell screamed *Drink!* I drank half the bottle straight down. In my desperation for moisture, I drank the rest.

I was all right for a minute or two, my thirst slaked, my head clear enough to think, This isn't a cool place to hang out. Ducking outside, I struck out along a track running between drystone walls, persuading myself nothing was wrong. A couple of hundred metres further and the effects of the fire-water started to hit me hard – my legs began to fail, my vision blurred and I realized I'd just swallowed some vicious homebrew.

I staggered on, fighting mutinous legs, and just when I thought I could beat the booze by sheer willpower, my legs folded and the ground came up and smacked me in the head.

I knelt where I'd fallen, tongue loose, thirstier than

ever. Cursing myself, I struggled to my feet, and like a man in a typhoon, pitched and swayed and finally staggered off the track, where I lay on my back in the long grass, sky spinning crazily, laughing at my stupidity. Without water I couldn't go on.

The sun hammered my head – I felt violently ill.

And then, just as I began to have visions of dying where I'd fallen, my bones picked clean by buzzards, I imagined I heard water – *water!* Not flowing but draining, sucking sounds as though plugs were being pulled in fields of bathtubs. Water! I got to my feet, raised my head above the remains of a wall, and saw sheep grazing. I realized they were making the sucking noise with their legs in the swampy ground. Dragging my carcass over the wall, I crawled in among the sheep and slid into the nearest hole. *Water!* Chilled bog champagne. I licked it off my hands and arms – pressed lumps of mossy sod into my mouth.

The sun was dipping, night falling fast. My head reeled and pounded – my body cried out for sleep.

I heard nightmarish goings-on in the night, birds swooping and cawing, flapping round my head. I fought them off long as I could, but they were everywhere – cloaked in black and flapping rock to rock, screeching as they feasted on Shelly's heart, Archie's hands and Ravi's soul.

When I woke, it was light and I was stiff and damp and cold. My head throbbed, my mouth was dry. I sucked a spongy ball of grass, pulled myself out of my boggy bed and was horrified to find a dead sheep in the next hole not three metres away, eyes plucked from bleeding sockets. Looking up, I saw a row of hooded ravens on the arm of a dead tree, watching me.

I walked for hours, head ringing, poisoned stomach burning. It was a hot summer's day and I hobbled along, stopping every once in a while to remove my shoes and cool my blistered feet in damp grass.

I walked all day, drifted into a waking sleepwalk. With the light fading I hit a deserted lane and followed it. As I walked, I felt myself being watched. Cows standing ankle-deep in mist gazed after me with huge eyes.

Something interesting ahead, outlined against the sunset. Approaching in the twilight, I saw it was a derelict church, echoing out of the past and overgrown with shrubs. Behind it, the remains of a cemetery dug into a slope, sunken headstones choked in ivy. One of the maps I'd studied had shown an isolated symbol for a church. Round the side of the ruin, a sensational discovery – a sea of blackberry bushes! I dropped my bag and waded in, plucking fat berries and filling my mouth until my belly was full and my hands bloody with juice. Back among the ruins I found scoops of water lying in gigantic leaves, bent them to my mouth and drank water that had never tasted as good or quenched as deep.

Night closed in. I stretched out beneath the stars, listening for ghosts.

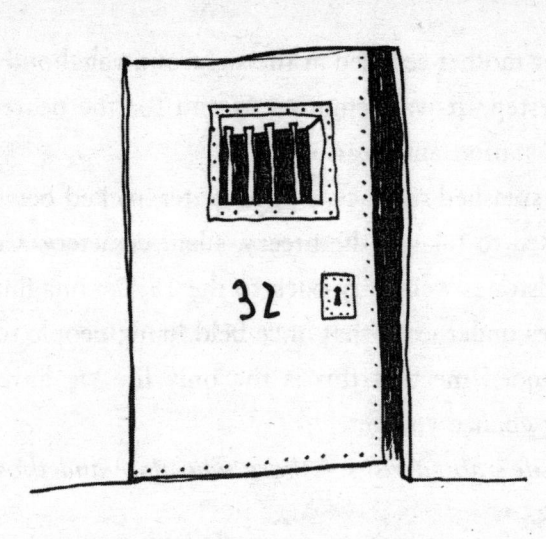

The sound of a tractor woke me. The sun was up. I lay on the hard ground, wondering why I felt so depressed, wishing I could go back to sleep and wake up excited. I lay there, asking myself why I wasn't celebrating. I'd escaped from Dovedale, remained free three whole nights and was confident I wasn't far from Salthaven.

But I didn't feel too sure about seeing Shannon. I'd only met her once and exchanged one brief letter. I didn't know if I could face her or anybody. Running away from anywhere can make you feel ashamed and isolated. You live by your wits and go into yourself, you become semi-wild and have difficulty talking to people. The great thing about the seaside and France was that nobody knew you, you could be anybody, you didn't have to mention running away. What if when I got there Shannon was busy – or wasn't there? What if her mother recoiled at the sight of a vagabond on her doorstep? It was tempting to aim for the nearest railway station and head south.

I splashed my face, sipped water, picked berries and paused to take in the breezy, silent cemetery. Crooked headstones went way back to the 1870s. Imagining the bones underneath that once held living people together reminded me that this is the only life we have – the only chance you get.

Life's about risks – those who dare and those who duck.

I headed back up the track to the lane. I was thinking about Shannon. Hard as I tried, I couldn't recall her face – only separate bits: her hazy eyes and slightly sticky-out ears, her pretty mouth and cool haircut.

The landscape wasn't as wild now. This was farmland. I could see the tractor working a field, pestered by seagulls. I thought I could hear the sea and limped faster. Climbed a stile, reached a high ridge and saw the *sea* below was a dual carriageway loaded with traffic. The maps I'd studied were either out of date or I was in the wrong neighbourhood. On the far side I could make out a pair of roadside restaurants.

Dropping down to the road, I waited for a gap in the traffic and sprinted to the grassy bank in the middle. Waited another hundred years, made it to the far side and headed for the restaurants. One of them was a standard glassy chain, the other an old truckers' shack with a blackboard saying ALL DAY BREKFAST and a fleet of trucks outside. Sauntered in. It was hot and steamy and jammed. A TV was on. The nearest table had a spare seat. I noticed a pay phone and started sorting coins. The truckers were a lively lot, talking loudly, slurping great mugs of tea. While I waited for my breakfast, I got up and phoned home with my back turned, twisting round to keep an eye on the TV mounted on the wall, praying there'd be nothing about me on the news. My mum answered and nearly freaked. I reassured her that everything was cool.

'Are you really OK, hon?'

'Why wouldn't I be – I'm free!'

She was afraid if I didn't turn myself in they'd send me down for good; she was afraid if I *did* turn myself in they'd send me down for good. She passed me on to my dad, who sounded more anxious than I'd ever heard him.

'Relax, Dad, I'm safe and on my way to a friend's house . . .' I was saying, when I saw the TV news had moved on to a local story, and found myself gazing at a familiar face on the screen, one looking curiously like me – and all at once I realized, That *is* me! The whole world was looking at that mugshot Mr Strang took my first morning in Dovedale after the barber massacred my dreadlocks. I gazed in horror – I looked tough and shifty, a typical young offender . . .

'Marcus? You there, Marcus?'

'It's OK, Dad, I gotta go – I'll call you soon as I can.'

'Hang on, Marcus, wait!'

'Tell Mum not to worry – everything's cool,' I hissed and hung up, and made my way back – head down and heart racing – to my place, where my breakfast was waiting.

I glanced up. My face had left the TV screen, and none of my fellow diners was taking any notice me, no one had made the connection between me and the face on the TV.

Or had they? Just as I was starting to eat, and telling myself not to wolf it this time, I felt eyes watching me; I looked up slowly and met the curious gaze of a trucker. I smiled and looked away. My appetite was blown. I paid and left.

Outside I gulped air and tried to think. A driver was climbing into the front of a truck. I ran over. 'Any chance of a lift, mate?'

He looked me up and down. 'Where you heading?'

'Salthaven.'

'All right, hop in.'

I climbed in. The driver had the radio on blasting out old hits.

'Is it far?' I asked as we bombed along.

'I wouldn't take you far. No insurance for hitchers. How old are you anyway?'

'Seventeen,' I said, skipping a year.

The news came on – another horrific suicide bomb,

freak floods across Europe, the latest obesity-busting diet from America . . . and in the local news, police were stepping up the search for runaway young offender Marcus King. I glanced at my driver. He was gazing at the road ahead; he'd heard it all before. Twenty minutes or so of silence later we rattled through a village and he said, 'Right, this is it – whereabouts?'

'This'll do fine.'

'It's all right, I'm not in a hurry.'

He got the address off me and stopped to ask directions – pitched the truck through a chain of new estates until a sign leaped out – GLENVIEW.

'Door-to-door service, pal,' he said, swinging the truck into a crescent with neat front gardens. I peered out at door numbers going by.

'Really appreciate it.'

I got down, waved to the driver as he pulled away. A gang of kids playing in the road stared at me. I smiled and pulled up my hood. Opened Shannon's gate and walked up to the door. I could hear a piano playing inside. Took a deep breath and rang the bell. Looked down at myself. Bloody hell.

The door opened. It was Shannon in a skirt, bare feet and a T-shirt saying CREDIBILITY GAP, gazing blindly at me. 'Hello?'

Such courage – I could've been anyone.

'Hi . . . it's me.'

'Marcus! I *knew* you'd come.'

Reaching for my hand, she pulled me inside and shut the door. We stood together, not saying anything. She was kind of looking at me, listening to my breathing, feeling my hands.

'It's OK, Marcus, you're safe now.'

'Sorry to bust in on you like this.'

'Don't be daft.'

She was alone. Her mum, a district nurse, was at work.

'What's the matter?'

'The door . . .'

'It's OK, I'll lock it.'

'Other way round – I usually like it open.'

'In case you want to escape from me too?'

'I know it's stupid, but—'

'Nothing's stupid,' she said, going to open it.

'It's OK, Shannon.' I stopped her. 'It's cool.'

She was still on holiday, planning to meet a friend. I said, 'Don't stop what you're doing for me.'

'Are you crazy?' she said, and called with some excuse.

She made us iced drinks and took me out the back, where we sat on the grass, facing each other, knees touching. There was so much I wanted to tell her, but I couldn't get started.

'Take your time,' she said, and the way she said it kind of uncorked me and I told her everything. She listened, her misty eyes on me, shocked when she heard how

254

Alice had been fired, and my coopmates hammered with six extra months. She was amazed at how I'd managed to stay off the Kalmasol, and how I'd discovered the Predator's secret – disgusted at the way he'd broken the deal, and tried to lock me in the slammer and how they wanted to up the meds again.

'It was war, Shannon – I had to get away.'

'I know, Marcus, I understand.'

'It's funny, isn't it?'

'What?'

'I've been running for ten years, and here I am, still running.'

She kind twisted up her mouth, and I knew I wasn't going to like whatever was coming.

'Don't suppose you kept that UN article you mentioned on the beach – the one slamming Britain's treatment of young offenders?'

I dug it out and read it her. She was thinking hard.

'Marcus, are you ready to blow the whistle on that place?'

'What you got in mind?'

'When we heard about your escape, my mum and I talked about you and I think she's right . . . it'd be crazy to keep running.'

'What are you saying?'

'It might be time to stop.'

'Shannon, that's like . . .'

I couldn't speak, I was gob-smacked.

'Marcus, if they recapture you—'

'What if they don't? What if I keep one step ahead of them?'

'That makes you a fugitive, forever looking over your shoulder.'

'What choice have I got?'

'Make a stand! Here, with me and my mum. Show them what a cool, responsible guy you are. Listen, I called the radio station and told them you were a friend of mine and you might be willing to talk about Dovedale – I hope you don't mind.'

'You talked to the press?'

'I didn't say where I was calling from. You angry?'

'With you?' I laughed and looked up at a formation of birds crossing high over a neighbouring field – geese or whatever heading south, I imagined, for warmer climes.

'Marcus, what you did trying to get the others off their meds and fighting the system and escaping was brilliant – it was fresh, it was new – but this running sounds like old stuff . . . like you're stuck in a groove – know what I mean?'

I remembered telling Archie something similar.

I let out a sigh. 'I thought a lot about what you said on the beach, Shannon, and decided you were right, it was my duty to shine a light on Dovedale. Trouble is, the minute I announce myself, they'll nab me – and I couldn't stand it, Shannon, courts and handcuffs, someone throwing a blanket over me and stuffing me into a police car in front of a million TV viewers . . .'

The birds heading south grew smaller and smaller.

'Marcus . . . can I say something?'

'Shoot.'

'Something you won't want to hear?'

I laughed nervously. 'Be as direct as you like!'

'You're going to hate me for this,' she said, finding my hand, 'but I think it might be best if you turn yourself in.'

'Turn myself in? Shannon, I just got out! I've just escaped from Alcatraz and crossed forty-five miles of wilderness to reach you.'

'I know, Marcus' – squeezing my hand – 'I know – believe me.'

'Shannon,' I whispered, 'I broke out of Dovedale to be free, to get back control of my life. Are you really asking me to . . . ?'

I couldn't bear it – swear to God, I couldn't bear it.

'Look, Marcus' – touching my face and leaving her hand on my cheek – 'if they recapture you, they're in control – but if you voluntarily turn yourself in, you are.'

I probably knew all along she was right, but we argued back and forth while I tried to get used to the idea of picking up a phone and saying, *Hi! Remember that young offender you were looking for . . . ?* It wasn't the kind of move I could have made on my own, or under the influence of Kalmasol. I needed help to kick the running habit.

I did turn myself in, but not before I'd spoken to a woman from the local paper at Shannon's house, and to someone from the BBC on the blower, who then hot-footed a reporter to Salthaven to make sure I was the genuine article. It was early September and there wasn't a lot happening in the news and all at once *I* was news, a second-string VIP.

The interviews were no easy rides. The reporters were friendly but suspicious. You could see it in the woman's eyes and hear it in the guy's voice – *You're just a bad egg with a smooth tongue, hyping up the horrors of Dovedale. You've run away* yet again *and you're looking for sympathy – or revenge.*

Shannon predicted this would happen. Without her I'd have got all worked up and maybe blown it – those guys can tie you up in knots – but she was like a manager talking me through the fight the night before: how to stay cool and not get provoked into exaggerated swipes, how to start slow and save the big hits till the end. In both cases I won them over gradually, and in both cases they also saved their best shots for the end. The local reporter, who came round with her photographer, looked at me thoughtfully and smiled.

'One more thing, Marcus – if the drugs are as disorienting as you say, how did you manage such a mentally and physically demanding escape?'

And the bloke from the BBC tried the same low hit from a different angle: 'If you don't mind my saying, Marcus, you're pretty calm and articulate for a guy on such debilitating medication.'

'You're right,' I told them. 'Being on Kalmasol is like wading through a bad dream, and yes, it would have affected my planning and slowed me right down. Only I haven't touched the stuff in weeks – twenty-three days, if you really wanna know,' and I introduced them to my chewing-gum trick.

They both wanted to know whether slogs really *had* to take the drugs?

'Are you joking?' I said, and explained what happened when you tried to resist. 'That's right, two of them held me down and prised open my mouth so the doctor could do his thing. With an audience, by the way – a full house.'

I was invited to discuss my Dovedale experience on some regional TV programme, but before I could go, the cops turned up to interview me. I was relaxed, my reasons for escape and my views on Dovedale calmly delivered. Shannon's mum served them tea and scones, strawberry jam and whipped cream. They weren't in any hurry to leave.

Then, just as I was getting really comfortable, they drained their cups and stood.

'OK, Marcus, time to go.'

Shannon and her mum begged them to let me stay, but it doesn't work that way. The system has to make its point, like a big dog that feels the need to put a troublesome mutt in its place.

I tried to sound cool, but inside I was dying – my nightmare scenario, dragged back to Hell Hall in disgrace. I needn't have worried. I was taken into youth custody, a medium-security home for wayward teenagers, where I signed a load of papers and promises, and the staff were cool and gave me my own little room – door ajar – and a key to the front door. No handcuffs, no heavies, just a couple of friendly social workers helping me sort out my future. Shannon was right, turning myself in was a smart move.

The interviews didn't seem to have much impact at first, but after a week or so reporters started showing up at Dovedale, and later someone asked a few awkward questions in Parliament, like: *Aside from the questionable use of medication as a means of control in young offenders' institutions, is the minister aware that* 200,000 *children and adolescents across the country are currently being prescribed Kalmasol?*

Over the next twelve months Miss Rice-Bird put up a vigorous defence of Dovedale and the government stuck to its guns: Dovedale and institutions like it were vital in order to protect the public and help rehabilitate troubled teenagers.

Clarence Trust was the first to resign his job, and the interviews he gave echoed mine. Pressure built up in the press; TV crews showed up at Dovedale from home and abroad. The Iceberg and the Predator hung on for another eighteen months until the government caved in and Dovedale was suddenly closed.

Over the next few years I managed to get in touch with my coopmates, all of whom – despite my public pleas – did their full six extra months in Dovedale. I went to visit Ravi in Highbury in North London, where he lives with his mum. He nearly did a double back-flip he was so happy to see me. He was seeing a counsellor and slowly coming off the meds. He's not working yet, but still dreams of running his own dot.com business. We hugged warmly and promised to keep in touch. I visited Archie in prison in Manchester. I don't think he really wanted to see me. He put on a big act, bragging about it all. He had burns all over his arms and he was pale and thin and never stopped clicking his fingers. I've never been so depressed in all my life. As for Shelly, he waved his family goodbye and went to the States, hung out in San Francisco for a time. He lives in Italy and keeps telling us to come out and stay, and we will one of these days.

Five years on and Shannon and I run a lively campaign over the net called CRAK – Concerned Relatives Against Kalmasol. We've got 13,000 paid-up members and our website gets fifty new hits a week – people concerned not just about side-effects, but the whole wacky notion of treating unhappy young people with mind-altering drugs. We get angry hits too, people swearing that Kalmasol is the answer to their prayers, that it's saved their children's lives and so on. Shannon always replies sympathetically, with me mumbling in the background – *Everybody's entitled to their opinion, however crazy.*

Shannon works for YAP – Youth Action Project – specializing in young people's rights. Me, I've never hit the big time, but I do a bit of DJing in local clubs and mixing for mates, and I've got the coolest music stall on Brixton Market.

We visited Dovedale the other day. Got the train to Gateshead and hired a car. We took our time – it was a beautiful day – spread a picnic on the edges of Strapps Wood, close to where the Hare and Hounds used to take off. Listen closely and you can still hear the echoes of panting slogs stopping to chalk up another arrow before running on.

It was a gas seeing the place again.

There's a smart spiked fence all round Dovedale now, which is ironic. The car park's been extended and the fountain's restored and working. It's called Dovedale Lodge and it's a hotel of sorts, a retreat for burned-out businessmen. Fishing, hunting, fitness programmes, psychotherapy, that kind of deal. I told the geezer on the gate I was a former inmate and would he mind if we went in and had a look, and he pretended to know nothing about Dovedale's previous life and said emphatically, *No!* Shannon persevered, and he finally agree to let us walk a short way in the grounds, provided he could see us and we didn't approach anyone. You could see his point. It might not be good for business were I to introduce myself to some jaded city dealer and tell him how his luxury bedroom used to be home to a brotherhood of medicated misfits like me.

I'd have loved to show Shannon the coop, and the classroom where Alice inspired us and Mr Kyte depressed us, and the dining hall where we used to line up for our dope, and Mr Strang's secret 'stockroom' and the good old slammer where I cracked the record.

Then all of a sudden it wasn't such a gas – a shiver

went through me, memories crashing in.

'You OK, Marcus?'

'Just for a second there . . .'

'What?'

'I thought I was back then . . . and this was all a dream.'

As we sat kicking our legs on the rim of the fountain it was getting towards sunset, and Dovedale stood out against the sky like it did that first night all those years ago when I arrived from London in handcuffs.

'When you first got here,' said Shannon, taking my hand, 'I bet you never thought that one day you'd be the first slog to get clean away from Dovedale, and also help blow it away.'

I laughed out loud. It was all too funny, too crazy. 'How did I ever end up here?'

'You were a bad boy, that's how,' she said. 'I should never have had anything to do with you.'

'You're right, I was a bad boy, I believed in free will. We've got a choice, I really believe that. You can let them snap the chains on your mind or you can say, *No! I'm free and you can't touch me!*'

With that I got up and grabbed hold of Shannon. 'Hey! What are you doing?' she laughed as I lifted her up, hitched her onto my back and galloped off with her down the field into Strapps Wood yelling, 'To be gloriously free, my friends . . . or to be one more sad zombie – that is the question!'